About Author

Michelle Vernal lives in Christchurch, New Zealand with her husband, two teenage sons and attention seeking tabby cats, Humphrey and Savannah. Before she started writing novels, she had a variety of jobs:

Pharmacy shop assistant, girl who sold dried up chips and sausages at a hot food stand in a British pub, girl who sold nuts (for 2 hours) on a British market stall, receptionist, P.A...Her favourite job though is the one she has now – writing stories she hopes leave her readers with a satisfied smile on their face. Visit Michelle at her website: www.michellevernalbooks.com

Also by Michelle Vernal

Michelle Vernal

The Guesthouse on the Green Series

Book 1 - O'Mara's

Book 2 – Moira-Lisa Smile

Book 3 –What goes on Tour

Book 4 – Rosi's Regrets

Book 5 – Christmas at O'Mara's

Book 6 – A Wedding at O'Mara's

Book 7 – Maureen's Song

Book 8 – The O'Maras in LaLa Land

Book 9 – Due in March

Book 10 – A Baby at O'Mara's

Book 11 – The Housewarming

Book 12 - out July 2022

Liverpool Brides Series

The Autumn Posy

The Winter Posy

The Spring Posy

The Summer Posy out March 28, 2022

Isabel's Story

The Promise

The Letter

and...

The Cooking School on the Bay

Second-hand Jane

Staying at Eleni's

The Traveller's Daughter

Sweet Home Summer

When We Say Goodbye

The Housewarming

The Guesthouse on the Green, Book 11

Michelle Vernal

Michelle Vernal Publishing Limited

Chapter One

Dublin, August 2001

A isling O'Mara-Moran was not a happy camper despite the fine summer's day bestowed upon Dublin by the weather gods. She'd smiled so hard that morning at the couple who were as awkward as their triple barrelled name —Brown-Moriarty-Lark—her face had ached. It still did. A stream of bad language had popped into her head, but as a hospitality professional and manager of O'Mara's guesthouse, she believed the guest or guests, in this case, were always right even when they were wrong.

In the case of the Brown-Moriarty-Larks, they were wrong.

She'd met their type before. The sort of people who'd moan if they won the lottery. They were booked into a cosy double room, and their bed was not lumpy; there hadn't been a Galaxy bar wrapper under it before they'd taken over the room either, and the tea was so Twinings not Barry's thanks very much. Of course, she'd not said any of this to their faces as she humoured their complaints with her plastic smile and promises to investigate.

The pair who were from Tralee had acted like landed gentry from the moment they'd arrived at the Georgian guesthouse overlooking St Stephen's Green. They'd picked holes in everything managing to rub Bronagh, Ita and Mrs Flaherty up the wrong way within hours of being in residence.

Bronagh had left them twiddling their thumbs for an unacceptable amount of time in reception. Mrs Flaherty's full Irish breakfast was too greasy and Ita's cleaning substandard. None of which was true apart from the bit about Ita. Her cleaning would have been substandard if Aisling hadn't kept a close eye on her.

When she'd not been dealing with the terrible twosome from Tralee, she'd been smoothing her staff's ruffled feathers. Then, to top it all off, Mr Fox, who lived in Iveagh Gardens behind the brick wall separating the guesthouse courtyard from the park, had paid them a visit. The contents of the rubbish bin had been strewn across the courtyard for Mrs Flaherty to find earlier. The cook's language had been ripe as she collared Aisling on her way down the stairs with Quinn, but mercifully, Quinn had stepped in and pacified the little, round woman who could have stepped from the pages of an old-fashioned nursery rhyme if not for her ability to turn the air blue when it came to the fox. It hadn't taken much. An understanding, sympathetic smile and a promise to board up the hole the creature had slipped through. They both knew their determined nocturnal visitor would only dig another, but Mrs Flaherty was a sucker for a pair of baby blues like Quinn's.

The Brown-Moriarty-Larks were booked into the guesthouse for four days, and they were currently on day three. Aisling's diplomatic skills had been sorely tested over the last seventy-two hours, and her apprehension over this morning hadn't helped matters. Quinn's intervention over Foxgate had been a godsend. This was also why she was relieved to see the back of the guesthouse for a few hours. She couldn't be doing with irate cooks, naughty foxes, demanding guests, or nice guests either, for that matter. Bronagh would manage to man the fort.

She clenched even harder as the reason for her current state of clenching everything clenchable loomed in front of her.

'I don't like hospitals,' she said to her husband Quinn. He'd been suffering through this rhetoric since she'd got up that morning. She'd have turned on her lucky Louboutin heels and gone back home to the guesthouse if he didn't have such a tight hold of her hand.

The ten-minute bus ride to the James Street hospital was easier than taking the car. They could taxi home afterwards if need be.

'I know. You've mentioned it.' Other men might have been terse, but not Quinn. He was a patient man. He had to be, living with not one but two O'Mara women, his wife and his sister-in-law, Moira. Actually, you could make that three if you counted baby, Kiera. In his opinion, it hadn't been a moment too soon when Tom, Moira's partner, had moved into the family apartment on the top floor of the guesthouse. The odds had needed evening up, and now it wasn't only himself who got told off for leaving the toilet seat up.

Aisling's step faltered as they approached the glass doors of St James's hospital through which an elderly woman pushing a walking frame had emerged. Another woman, her daughter Aisling presumed, was bringing up the rear carrying an overnight bag. Somewhere, someone was smoking, the smell of cigarettes tangible but the culprit hidden.

The buildings sprawled around the hospital's modern entrance were a hodgepodge of old and new. Inside, Aisling visualised a hive of activity like on the tele. She was partial to flopping on the couch to watch the drama unfold on ER, although it wasn't the same since George had left. Life and death played out within these hospital walls every single day, she thought dramatically before informing Quinn, 'It's the smell. I hate it.' She pulled what her sisters called her liver and onions face to prove her point.

'Sure, you were grand visiting Moira in the hospital when she had Kiera, Ash. You'll be grand now,' Quinn stated as he continued to stride determinedly towards the entrance. Given the circulation to Aisling's hand was in danger of being cut off, she'd no choice but to keep walking. Quinn, on the whole, was an easy-going man, but today he was putting her in mind of a bossy Ronan Keating. Normally she'd have found this masterful version of her very own Ronan lookalike sexy enough to give him the glad eye but not today. Today there'd be no riding, thanks very much.

Her little legs were spinning like windmills trying to keep up and her heels tapping on the asphalt. 'Only because it was the new mammy ward Moira was on, and it smelled all yummy and talcum powdery. I like the new mammy ward. It's a happy place.' She longed to be on the new mammy ward herself and hoped she'd wind up there sooner rather than later after this morning. Time was ticking when it came to her biological clock, and although she tried her best, it was hard not to allow her desire—no, scratch that, it was a need to be a mammy—to swallow her up. The clock was always there inside her head, tick, tick, ticking, and it was getting deafening.

Quinn was trying to jolly her up, she knew this, but she was in no mood for being jollied up. She'd a feeling the words 'soldier on' would be next out of his mouth, and she wouldn't be responsible for her actions if they did trip off his tongue. It had been a favourite catchphrase of Mammy's. Indeed she'd use the same tone Quinn just had when Aisling had been a school girl feigning an upset tummy to get out of the cross country.

'Soldier on, Aisling,' she'd order. It was very annoying. Worst of all, though, was when she'd sing the song. It was a made-up Mammy song set to the tune of 'When The Saints Go Marching In'.

She began to hum under her breath.

Oh, soldier on, oh, soldier on,

Get out of bed, get out of bed,

Oh, soldier on, get out of bed,

Aisling, I want you off to schoo-oo-ool,

No child o' mine's gonna play me for a foo-ool

So, soldier on and get off to school.

Ah Jaysus, no! She'd have it stuck in her head all day now.

She hadn't wanted to soldier on or run. What she had wanted to do was lie in bed reading her book while her mammy brought her tea and toast. 'Running's the best medicine for an upset tummy, so it is. And you're not the only one who has to wear the romper shorts.' The curtains would be flung open, and Mammy would declare it a grand day for the cross country. It managed to rain every other day in Dublin but come the cross country day, you could put money on it being a scorcher.

Aisling didn't know what was worse. The never-ending run, the point of which she'd never ascertained, or having to squeeze into the brown romper shorts that Sister Bernadette said weren't all that dissimilar to the kit of an Olympian. She'd always drop this into her pep talk as they all lined up for the on yer marks, get set bit with their pale, goose-pimply flesh on display. But, unfortunately, Aisling felt nothing like an Olympian and more like a human chocolate éclair as she puffed and panted along, the rompers the colour of the icing and her legs the choux pastry.

Actually, she thought, today was a little like the cross country. She didn't want to participate, and as such, the idea of what was to come had become a big deal; however, she was resigned to having to go knowing there'd be a kind of euphoria when it was over. The only difference was she'd not be getting red in the face and sweaty, and Sister Bernadette wouldn't be there waving them in with her flag.

Mind you, sweaty was a possibility if Quinn didn't slow down and, ah, no, she thought, glancing down, she was even wearing a brown dress. Granted, it was a stylish linen shift, a long way from the polyester rompers but still and all, it was brown. She'd opted to wear a dress because it was easy to whip up or off, whichever was required of her. She'd chosen her knickers carefully too, opting for the aubergine sateen ones. Moira insisted on calling them her eggplant knickers on the rare occasions she folded the washing. They afforded full bottom coverage and boasted no saucy embellishments, sensible without being fugly. She wanted to strike the right chord in case it was like when you had the smear test, and you just dropped your drawers there on the ground and stepped out of them.

Quinn raised his eyebrows. 'Why are you humming 'When the Saints Go Marching In'?'

'Don't ask.'

'And, I don't recall talcum powder. Flowers, a sorta greasy, meaty soup smell I couldn't pinpoint and howling babies, is what I remember. Oh, and it was far too hot as well. Like being in the fecking tropics.' He squeezed Aisling's hand. 'You'll be grand. It's a quick procedure. There's nothing to it. Be grateful you won't have to stay in overnight and swelter while eating the greasy, meaty smelly soup.'

Aisling refused to smile. 'It's not you who's off to have a hosepipe up your whatsit, is it?'

Quinn winced. 'Aisling, it's called a catheter. You've had what's going to happen today explained to you by Doctor Kinsella, and Tom went through it all with you again last night. It's a straightforward procedure, and we'll be on our way home before you know it. You took two paracetamol like Tom suggested, didn't you?'

Aisling nodded. She was tempted to tell her husband to feck off with himself. She'd seen him when he'd had a teeny tiny sniffle. Anyone would have thought he was on his last legs with the flu. A blow by blow account of each drip of his nose he'd given her. Oh yes, it was alright for him with his yo-ho-ho styled you'll be on your way home before you know it.

Tom had indeed run through what would happen today with her, and Aisling was grateful for her sister's partner's patience. Moira had picked well in Tom. Not only did he have the best bum in Dublin, but he'd also make a grand GP one of these days. She'd told him as much when he'd given her a reassuring smile like a proper, qualified doctor would.

As for Moira, she'd received a scowl when she'd looked up from where she was feeding Kiera to say, 'Lie back and think of Ireland, Ash. Sure, it'll be a doddle compared to the childbirth. That's like having a hot poker up—' Aisling had cut her off and told her she wasn't being helpful.

Roisin hadn't been much better either. She'd rung from her flat in London to wish her luck for tomorrow's appointment and commenced with the Darth Vader breathing demonstration she was fond of rolling out in times of emotional need. Aisling had held the phone away from her ear. Roisin, as a yoga teacher in training in between being a mum to Noah and working as a secretary, was convinced the Darth Vader breathing fixed everything.

Aisling had squished up next to Moira on the sofa once Rosi had stopped her live demo so as Moira could say hello. She filled her eldest sister in on her niece, who was now a bonny five months old before Moira turned the topic to Aisling.

'Do you have any special breathing for angry people? Because Aisling got very angry at Quinn the other night. She threw a tea towel at him and told him he was a selfish —'

'Moira!' Aisling wrenched the phone from her sister.

'You and Quinn had a row?' Roisin asked. 'But you never row.'

'It wasn't really a row because it was only me doing the shouting. And I apologised for it. The anger bubbled up inside me.' She'd thundered as they did the washing up that he wasn't as invested in having a baby as she was because the restaurant was his baby, and Quinn's bistro did consume his time and energy, but he'd promised to delegate more when they became parents. He hadn't deserved her eruption though or getting a soggy tea towel chucked at him. 'I don't know, Rosi. If I'm not angry, then I'm tearful.'

Roisin launched into a round of breathing designed to calm and restore inner equilibrium, and when she was satisfied her sister had the hang of it, she voiced a concern of her own. Noah's pet gerbil. Apparently, his behaviour toward the new boy, erm gerbil, on the block was antisocial. 'Mr Nibbles is bullying Steve. He keeps sitting on him so he can't move like. It's not kind. I mean, I know Steve's a bit different. There's the lazy eye, for starters. I think Colin must have got him for a discounted price at the pet store—'

'Cheap, chinless feck,' Moira instantly piped up about her oldest sister's ex-husband.

Roisin didn't argue. 'But it's no excuse for picking on the poor fella, now is it? We should celebrate our differences.'

'Feck off with you, Rosi,' Aisling and Moira chimed in.

Rosi, unperturbed, carried on, 'I'm worried Mr Nibbles is sending the wrong signal to Noah.'

'Catch yourself on, Rosi,' Aisling said. 'He's hardly likely to go to school and start sitting on the other children. So don't be worrying about it.' A smile twitched at the imagery this conjured.

'Well, if you ask me, I think it's karma, Rosi,' Moira stated.

'I didn't ask you, and what do you mean?'

'Youse two.' Moira elbowed Aisling in the side. 'You used to sit on me all the time.'

'That was different.' The sisters were put out.

'How?'

'We've not got the lazy eye for starters,' Roisin said, and Aisling rubbing her side giggled and added, 'And you were a proper tell-tale tit always running to Mammy.'

'You were,' Roisin agreed. 'You deserved to be flattened. Poor Steve's an innocent. He doesn't do anything, and Mr Nibbles launches on him from the top of the spinning wheel. He's like a bat swooping, so he is.'

A thought occurred to Moira, who'd had enough of hearing about Mr Nibbles' bad behaviour. 'Ash, have you told Mammy about what you're after having done tomorrow? She'd want to know.'

'No, I have not and don't you be telling her either. She'll only say what's for you won't pass you by, and I'm in no mood for the rundown on the housewarming party either. Jaysus wept; it's not until the end of the month. That's three whole weeks of her going on and on about the fecking thing. She's acting as though she's hosting the queen's annual garden party, and besides, you know what she's like. If she caught wind of my procedure, she'd be standing on the main road in Howth like she was running for the council, with a loudspeaker informing strangers her daughter's after having the hosepipe up her whatsit first chance she got. Mammy loves a good medical procedure to broadcast, so she does. Remember how she dined out for weeks on us all thinking Patrick had a nasty boil on his neck, but it turned out to be an ingrown hair that had to be surgically removed.'

'Ah no, don't, Ash. I've not long had dinner,' Roisin muttered. 'You're right, though. Patrick was mortified. I wonder if Cindy knows that story?' Buxom, blonde Cindy, a star in waiting and their elder brother's fiancée over there in Los Angeles floated to mind.

'Bound to. She's met Mammy, hasn't she?' Aisling said.

'You're right. Do you remember that first boyfriend of mine, Kelly?'

'That's a girl's name.' Moira said.

'Smelly Kelly, terrible BO. I remember,' Aisling said. Now that she thought about it, Rosi's track record with men was not good. Shay, with whom she was conducting a long-distance Dublin to London love affair being the exception. He'd good hygiene habits and a chin, so hopefully, he was a keeper.

'That's him. Mammy collared him and told him all about the wart I had on my foot and how I cried when the doctor applied the dry ice on it. It was never the same between us after that. I think he saw a big warty foot every time he looked at me.'

Moira chimed in with how she'd suffered through a blow by blow account of Donal's recent fungal infection in his big toe, as well as the latest on who was coming to the Howth house party of the year. 'Mammy told him he's to wear the flip-flops and let the air at it. She wants it sorted by the time the party rolls around.'

'Three weeks for him to get rid of it then,' Roisin said. 'She wants me and Noah to come over, you know.'

'Well, it's only fair you should have to suffer through it too.' Moira said. 'And besides, you're due to see Kiera. She's grown loads, hasn't she, Ash? It would be grand to get the two cousins together too.'

'She's grown loads,' Aisling confirmed.

'So you're coming?' Moira asked.

'I suppose so. I'm desperate to see Kiera, so's Noah. We can stay with Shay.'

'Grand, it'll be a gas.' Aisling said.

'No, it'll be shite.' Moira moved back to the toenail business. 'I asked Tom if fungal toe infections are contagious, and he says no, but I'm not convinced. It was very distracting when Donal took me for my driving lesson. I kept glancing down at the manky thing making sure he was keeping it on his side of the car.'

'I'm surprised she hadn't slathered it in the E45 cream,' Roisin said.

'She did, but he's a prescription from the doctor now because the cream only made it greasy and fungally. God help us if he ever gets the piles,' Moira added. 'Especially now Mammy's got that new whiz-bang camera she's forever waving in Kiera's face.'

In London, Rosi pulled the liver and onion face, as did Aisling. The sisters knew Mammy was fond of photographic evidence of medical complaints and was apt to wave them about as a doctor would an X-ray.

'You alright there, Aisling?' Quinn asked, pulling her back from her thoughts as the glass doors of St James's hospital slid open.

'I will be so long as Donal never gets the piles.'

Chapter Two

'Aisling, what's with the breathing thing? You look like you're in difficulty. You'll have the ER attendants rushing over with the oxygen if you keep it up.'

Aisling didn't know when she'd stopped humming the soldier on song and begun the heavy breathing. 'It's the Darth Vader breathing. Rosi swears by it for calming you down.' Aisling mouthed, 'I'm fine' to the nurse who was eyeballing her as though she were an escaped patient. She'd a brown paper bag in her hand stained with grease. It was lucky Mammy wasn't here, Aisling thought because she'd tell yer nurse wan she wasn't setting a good example with her food choices and her working in the hospital and all.

She needed another wee, she realised with a jiggle and casting about spied the stick figure woman in a skirt, but there was a yellow cleaning sign propped up on the floor outside the door.

Quinn tracked her gaze. 'You went right before we left.'

'I know, but I always need to wee when I'm uptight and believe me, I'm very, very uptight.'

Quinn squeezed her hand. 'We'll find you another toilet once we figure out where to go.' He marched up to the reception desk, and Aisling looked back over her shoulder. There were people seated near the hospital entrance, and her eyes flitted from an elderly couple holding hands to a teenage girl with her arm in a cast whose mother was wearing an expression of annoyance. A doctor with a stethoscope slung around his neck breezed through, and disappointingly he looked more like Bill Murray than George Clooney. She turned back to the receptionist, who was gesturing toward the lifts. The underlying odour of pine-scented disinfectant was burning her nostrils, and she wished she were anywhere but here.

She tried to conjure up the smell of Kiera when she'd held her earlier. Not when she'd filled her nappy, obviously, but after, when she'd had her bottle and was all sweet and milky. She loved her baby niece so much it made her ache sometimes. She loved Noah too, of course. He could always be relied upon to make her smile. She wished she could have a quick chat with him now, but he'd be at school, hopefully not sitting on his fellow pupils.

'Come on, Ash, this way.' Quinn steered her towards the lift, where they stood alongside an orderly with an hospital bed to await it.

Aisling's mobile began to ring.

'Leave it,' Quinn said. 'Whoever it is can wait.'

'But it might be important.' Aisling could never ignore a ringing phone. She stepped away from the lift and unzipped her bag, rummaging around until she found her mobile. 'Hello, this is Aisling.'

'Aisling, this is your mammy.' The voice was shrill in Aisling's ear. 'I'm on my mobile phone, can you hear me?'

'Loudly and clearly, Mammy.' She held the phone a little distance from her ear.

'Holy Mary Mother of Jesus, what's all this about a hysterectomy?' There was a note of hysteria in the question.

Fecking Moira, Aisling frowned.

'Aisling?'

'I'm here. Jaysus, Mammy. I'm not having a hysterectomy.' Aisling turned her back on the orderly who was scratching a spot on his chin. The lift pinged its arrival, and the doors slid open.

'C'mon, Ash,' Quinn urged. 'Ring her back.'

'What are you having then?' Maureen O'Mara's voice was slightly calmer, but only just. 'And so as you know, I'm wounded that a child of my flesh and blood didn't see fit to tell me she was going to the hospital. Wounded I am.'

Instead of pushing the bed into the lift, the orderly hung back to eavesdrop.

'I'm having a hysterosalpingogram,' Aisling said this slowly to be sure her mammy heard her correctly. 'And I didn't tell you because I didn't want to worry you.' A white and necessary lie.

The orderly, unimpressed, trundled the bed into the lift. 'You coming, mate?' he asked Quinn.

Quinn nodded and stepped inside, holding the door open with one hand and pulling Aisling in alongside him with the other.

'And what's that then? Is it life-threatening? It sounds terrible, so it does. I should be by your side, Aisling. It's a Mammy's place.' Her voice was rising, and Aisling pictured her shouting down the phone the whole family wished she'd never got the hang of.

'No, calm down, Mammy. It's not life-threatening. It's a simple procedure to see if there's a blockage in my fallopian tubes because if there is, it could be stopping Quinn and me from conceiving. Sure, I can go back to work straight after if I feel up to it. No big deal.' Her blasé tone belied her anxiety even though she knew it was a straightforward procedure and not open-heart surgery she was going to be having. She expected some cramping afterwards and to wear a pad. The after-effects though were considered minor. She had cramping now from all the clenching. Her poor bottom cheeks were going to be sorer than her nether regions at this rate.

'I see, and who's going to be doing the unblocking of your falutin tubes?'

'A radiologist.'

'Put him on then. Tell him your mammy's wanting a word.'

'Mammy, I—'

The phone was snatched from her hand.

'Maureen, it's Quinn here. We're going to be late for Aisling's appointment. She'll ring you when it's done to let you know how she gets on.'

A tinny voice bellowed out of the phone.

Quinn, however, was in full bossy Ronan Keating mode now. 'No, Maureen, listen. Like she said, it's nothing for you to worry about.' He disconnected the call and then switched the mobile off.

Aisling found Quinn extremely attractive at that moment.

Over on Howth Pier, Maureen O'Mara stared at her Nokia for a moment. She didn't know who had her feeling more vexed. Quinn for hanging up on her or Moira. How she could get a hysterectomy confused with her sister having a hyster whatever it was, was beyond her. She'd been having palpitations that Aisling was about to undergo life-changing surgery without her mammy having the foggiest.

A fine doctor's wife Moira would make one day, she humphed to herself, shoving the phone in the pocket of her Mo-pants. Then, spying a woman walking toward her with a black cocker spaniel on a lead, her eyes lit up. She made a beeline for her. While Pooh gave happy poodly yaps introducing himself to the cocker spaniel, Maureen announced, 'Would you believe my daughter's after having a hysterectomy to see if her falutin tubes are blocked, and I'm the last to hear about it?'

Chapter Three

Aisling stared up at the ceiling from where she lay prone on the X-ray table. Quinn's stomach rumbled, sounding loud in the room, and he mumbled an apology. She tightened the death-like grip she had of his hand. The lights were super bright, and closing her eyes, yellow spots danced on the inside of her lids.

The radio-whatsit people, a man and a woman in white coats, were doing their best to put her at ease, and Aisling didn't want them to feel as though they weren't doing a good job, so she took a deep breath and tried to relax. Thirty minutes was all it would take. She could do this. Lie back and think of Ireland, Aisling.

She'd told her mammy this procedure was no big deal. A big, fat lie if ever there was one because this whole trying to have a baby was a very big deal. It had become a bigger deal as Aisling's period had arrived like an unwelcome guest showing up on the doorstep month after month despite her careful temperature taking and timetabled rides.

She'd tried hard to keep perspective. Sure, she was always hearing stories about how once couples struggling to conceive stopped making having a baby their number one focus, it just happened. So she'd stopped pestering Quinn for sex every five minutes when she was ovulating. She no longer mentioned her yearning to be a mam to anyone who cared to listen, and she'd quashed all those ugly, green emotions she'd felt when Moira had got pregnant without even trying. She was doing her best to get on with things, but it was hard, especially when there seemed to have been a baby boom in Dublin. Everywhere she looked these days, she saw women ripe in pregnancy or pushing prams and, it was always there, the fear. The 'what if' fear.

What if she couldn't get pregnant? What then?

Aisling was good at putting a cheery face on things though. Her years in hospitality had taught her the show must go on no matter what. And it had, until the sixteenth of July when she'd woken to a familiar dull ache. She'd staggered off to the bathroom to sort herself out and then had crawled back into bed feeling despair so crushing she'd pulled the covers over her head and stayed there.

Quinn had gone to the gym, and Moira, caught up sorting Kiera, didn't realise her sister hadn't gone downstairs to start her working day. It was Bronagh who sent up the SOS that Aisling was MIA.

Aisling didn't care that she was needed downstairs. She was too tired to speak to anyone. All she wanted to do was sleep and shut out the fear.

Moira, Tom, Quinn and Bronagh had other ideas though.

Moira kicked things off by making Kiera do cute things beside the bed, but Aisling burrowed further under the bedding, ignoring them both. Alarmed, the youngest O'Mara filled Tom in and then rang down and reported to Bronagh. The receptionist suggested Snowballs, but unfortunately, Moira had helped herself to Aisling's chocolate marshmallow stash and had failed to replenish it. So instead, custard creams from Bronagh's personal supply were sent up, and while Moira ate four thanks to the stress Aisling was causing her, Aisling herself was not tempted.

After initial reluctance to enter his sister-in-law's bedroom, Tom ventured in to speak to her, but she wouldn't tell him what was wrong. 'I think she might be depressed. She doesn't want to talk to me, so I think she should go and see her GP,' he said, giving his verdict to Moira, who muttered, 'I'll give her something to be depressed about.' She hot-footed it off to her and Tom's room and reappeared wearing the Bono mask she'd saved from Aisling's hen night, an in-joke because Aisling was not a fan of the Irish rocker.

The sight of his wife with Bono's face put the fear of God up Tom and silenced Kiera's grizzling. But, when Moira wrenched back Aisling's bed covers and threatened to play the Rattle and Hum album over and over if she didn't get up, Aisling merely blinked at her. Kiera, however, howled at the prospect.

Quinn returned, sweaty from his workout, to be collared by a panicking Moira, and after his initial fright at the Bono mask, he was all ears as she told him she'd done her best to get his wife out of bed, but now it was down to him. First, he tried cajoling Aisling to no avail, then decided to do what he did best. Make food. Not even the whiff of chocolate brownie moved her though, and that was when it was agreed it was time to call in the big guns. Maureen.

Moira held the phone to Aisling's ear as their mammy launched into the Soldier On song, only she swapped out school for work. It had the desired effect, that and the threat of a visit. The prospect of her mammy coming over to personally drag her out of her bed was enough to penetrate the fog around Aisling's brain and get her moving.

She showered, dressed, and Quinn marched her off to her doctor, having made an urgent appointment.

'Aisling,' Doctor Kinsella had looked at her kindly from behind her glasses, 'I'm going to ask you a few questions to try and get to the bottom of what had you feeling like you didn't want to face the world this morning, alright?'

Aisling nodded. She liked Doctor Kinsella. She was the sort of doctor who still gave children lollipops when they had an injection.' Quinn squeezed her hand.

'Is getting pregnant something you think about all the time?'

A big nod.

'And the fact it's not happening is making you sad?'

She could feel Quinn's eyes on her as she gave a slight nod and felt guilty. She should have told him how she'd been feeling. They were supposed to share things with each other. But by voicing her worries, she'd have made them real because it was an acknowledgement there might be a problem.

'And angry,' Quinn added helpfully. 'Very angry.'

Doctor Kinsella jotted something down on her pad. 'And, have you been doing numerous pregnancy tests throughout each month?'

A wary nod. Christ on a bike, she'd peed on more sticks than the Pope had given blessings these last months.

And so it went on until Doctor Kinsella got to the good bit, the fixing it bit. Given they'd been doing everything right with timing her ovulation without success for the last six months, she was going to send them off to St James's for what was called a hysterosalpingogram. 'This is the next step, that's all, Aisling. I'm not saying there is a problem. Do you understand?'

She bobbed her head again.

'It's early days. There's no reason to assume that things won't happen in due course.'

Aisling knew this but each month that passed felt like another nail in the coffin. Quinn relaxed slightly on the seat next to her, his grasp of her hand loosening a little as he asked. 'So what exactly is a hyster—'

'Hysterosalpingogram,' Doctor Kinsella finished before explaining the procedure to them. She tapped away at her computer for a minute or two, then swivelled around in her chair to face them once more.

'What do you enjoy doing, Aisling?'

'Erm, eating.'

Doctor Kinsella smiled, 'No, I mean with your spare time. Hobbies and the like.'

'We don't have much in the way of spare time.' She glanced at Quinn. It was true. She split her time between O'Mara's and the restaurant. They were busy people who were always on the go. It was like that when you ran a business. 'I used to like reading though.' She couldn't remember the last time she'd curled up with a good book and whiled away an hour or two.

'And we did the salsa dancing lessons, don't forget,' Quinn added so as they didn't sound like a pair of complete workaholics. 'It was how we got together.'

Aisling raised a smile at the memory of Quinn's fancy footwork across the dance studio floor, which had ended with a first kiss.

'I see,' Doctor Kinsella said, her hands clasped in front of her and resting on her desk, which could do with a tidy up. 'Well, I think it's important you slow down a little. Take some time to relax. Not just Aisling, you as well, Quinn.'

'Take a holiday, you mean?' Quinn asked.

'No, not necessarily, but, Aisling, pick up a book and make time to sit and read it. Or, go for a walk together, see a film, and you said you did salsa dancing lessons?'

They both nodded. 'We were good, weren't we?' Aisling said.

'We were,' Quinn agreed.

'Well, why not start them up again?'

'We could, couldn't we,' Quinn said.

'We could,' Aisling said.

Doctor Kinsella looked pleased. 'Stop worrying, Aisling, and take this one step at a time.'

Aisling raised her eyes to meet her doctor's reassuring gaze. She was going to have a test that would show if there were any problems with her fallopian tubes and if there were, it would be addressed. She wasn't a lost cause.

The exhaustion that had dogged her that morning was beginning to ease like the sun dispersing a morning fog because hope was a powerful thing.

Aisling opened her eyes, realising she was being spoken to. 'Nearly done, how you doing there?'

Thank the Lord for that. 'I'm fine.' Aisling managed.

Chapter Four

I t was lunchtime when Aisling and Quinn left the hospital. Aisling was giddy with relief at the procedure being over and done with. It had been uncomfortable and undignified despite the professionalism of the two radio-whatsits. She'd got through it though and was stood outside St James's blinking into the bright sunshine. There was nothing else for it now but to wait to hear what the results were.

'Shall we get a taxi back to O'Mara's, and you can put your feet up for a few hours?' Quinn asked anxiously as he took in his wife's pallor beneath the cloud of hair. The sun was making it look more gold than red this afternoon. 'You're a little pale.'

'I'm Irish, aren't I? And, sure, I'm grand. Don't fuss so.' Her voice was a little shorter than it should have been, given he was only looking out for her wellbeing. It was just ever since the sixteenth of July he'd been looking out for her wellbeing a little too much.

She did feel fine, not so much as a hint of the cramps she'd been warned about. It was such a gorgeous day, too nice to go straight back to the guesthouse she thought as the sun caressed her. It was the sort of day on which you should take a stroll with your husband. Of course, she never played hooky and nor did Quinn, but there was always a first time for everything.

O'Mara's was in the capable hands of Bronagh and she'd cope with the terrible two from Tralee if need be. Since time began, the receptionist had worked the front desk of

O'Mara's and had seen her fair share of Brown-Moriarty-Lark types come and go. She was adept at managing their more difficult guests with aplomb.

Besides, the disagreeable couple shouldn't be back for ages yet. Aisling had enthusiastically waved them off on a tour of Glendalough before she and Quinn had left for the hospital. With any luck, Fergus, their tour guide, would abandon them in the wilds of Wicklow to never be heard from or seen again. If, however, Fergus did return them safely to the guesthouse, she'd be back long before their new night receptionist, Freya took over from Bronagh.

Aisling had been sad to lose Nina. The Spanish girl was reliable and had a lovely manner with the guests along with a kind heart, but she was glad she was home with her daughter where she belonged. As for Freya, well, Aisling had mixed feelings. She was doing her best to give the twenty-two-year-old she was related to in a second or third cousin sorta way the benefit of the doubt, and it was early days, but so far, so good. Just because her mother, Emer, was the family's black sheep didn't mean she was tarred with the same brush. At least she hoped it didn't. It did mean she'd felt she had to give her the job though.

At Quinn's, the lunch service at the restaurant would be in full swing now but his staff would have everything under control. There was no reason they shouldn't take a few more hours off, she decided, biting the bullet.

'Listen, why don't we pick up sandwiches and go and have lunch in the Green?' She suddenly wanted nothing more than to stretch out on the warm grass and bask in the sunshine for a few hours with her husband by her side. If Quinn made noises about needing to get back to work, she'd hit back with a picnic at St Stephen's Green being good for her wellbeing because Dr Kinsella had said so, more or less. He'd not argue with her.

There was no need though. Quinn agreed that sounded a grand way to while away an hour or two.

'I'd best get ringing Mammy out the way. Phone please.' She held her hand out for the mobile her husband had commandeered in the lift.

Quinn dug it out of his pocket. 'She won't be happy with me for cutting her off. Put in a good word.'

'I'll not be her favourite daughter either.'

'Good luck.' He pressed the phone into her palm, and they shared a complicit smile.

Aisling bit her lip. Right get this over with. She listened to the phone ring, holding it a little away from her ear as her mammy's voice suddenly bellowed out.

'Hello, you're speaking with Maureen O'Mara on her mobile phone.'

'Mammy, it's me, Aisling.'

'Aisling! It's Aisling, Bernadette.'

'Who's Bernadette?' Aisling asked. 'And you don't need to shout. I can hear you.'

'My new friend. We met on the pier this morning, walking the dogs after that husband of yours hung up on me. We've loads in common, and I'm after inviting her to the housewarming. I'm delighted to say she's said she'll come.'

'We were going to be late for the appointment, Mammy.' Aisling shot a glance at Quinn, who grinned unrepentantly back at her. 'He'd no choice but to cut you off.'

'Lateness is no excuse for being rude. Manners are next to godliness, Aisling.'

Aisling dodged a young woman hurrying past and was surprised to see she didn't have a trail of bees buzzing behind her, given she smelled like a giant flower. 'He wasn't rude.'

'I wasn't rude, Maureen,' Quinn called out. 'Not on purpose.'

Maureen decided to move on. The initial panic over Aisling's hospital visit had receded, and she was feeling more magnanimous towards her son-in-law. And sure, every cloud had a silver lining, didn't it because hadn't she met Bernadette? 'Pooh's getting on great guns with Mirabelle, Bernadette's cocker spaniel.' There'd been an embarrassing moment where he'd forgotten he no longer had his bits and had tried to have his way with poor Mirabelle, who'd looked very let down over it all but she and Bernadette had laughed and said, 'Dogs will be dogs.

'We're after having coffee and a slice of the millionaire's shortbread you're fond of in the café near the pier. You know the one with yer man who looks like a pirate.'

Aisling's mouth watered at the thought of the rich caramel-filled slice. She was starving. 'Well, I rang to tell you it's over and done with, and I'm fine, so you're not to worry.' This was when her Mammy should say goodbye and hang up, she thought. But no, this was Mammy she was dealing with. Aisling heard her inhale, ready to settle in for a good chinwag.

'I told Bernadette you've decided to investigate whether there are any problems with your womanly bits by having a hysterectomy. She's been worried about you too. We've both been waiting for you to call so we have.'

'Jaysus wept, Mammy. It was a hysterosalpingogram,' Aisling shouted, oblivious to the startled glances she was on the receiving end of. She'd have liked to have told her mammy that she didn't appreciate her sharing her and Quinn's personal business with a stranger too but knew she'd be wasting her breath.

'Don't shout, Aisling. I can hear perfectly well, thank you. And that's what I said. Now, how are you? Did it hurt?'

Aisling rolled her eyes. 'No, not really. I mean, it wasn't pleasant, but like I said, I'm fine, Mammy. Quinn and I are strolling, as I speak, towards St Stephen's Green. We're going to have a picnic lunch.'

'She's up and about Bernadette, off for a picnic no less. The hyster-thing-a-me-jig didn't hurt either, which is good because Aisling's pain threshold is non-existent. You want to have heard the carry on when she grazed her knee as a child or the like. You'd have thought she'd been orphaned and abandoned on the streets of Dublin to fend for herself.'

'I wasn't that bad.'

'Yes, you were. When will you hear?'

'The results of the examination should be in within a few days.'

'And what if your falutin tubes are blocked? What then?'

'Fallopian tubes, and can we talk about this when I'm not traipsing along a public pavement, Mammy?' There were several possibilities as to what would happen next. Fertility medication was an option if one of her tubes was blocked and the other in good working order. Or, if both were blocked, surgery to open them was likely.

'It's not the nineteen fifties, Aisling. People know babies aren't a result of immaculate conception. Things aren't all hush-hush like they used to be. Bernadette's daughter was having trouble getting in the family way too. So you're not alone. I told her it wasn't for lack of trying on yours and Quinn's part. Ten out of ten for effort because, according to Moira, you're at it all the time.'

'Mammy!' She'd definitely be sitting on Moira when she got home. Aisling knew better than to ask, but she couldn't help herself. 'And did Bernadette's daughter get pregnant then?' For reasons she couldn't fathom, it felt important that she had. That she'd had a happy ending in her quest to become a mammy.

'Yes, she did. She had the IUD treatment and wound up with twins. But, sadly, her eejit husband couldn't cope and left her.'

'IVF, Maureen,' a stranger's voice corrected in the background.

Maureen ignored her new friend. 'You'll be relieved to have it done and dusted.'

'I am. Listen, I'd better go, Mammy.'

'Right well, call me later when you're at home and give me the proper rundown like.'

Aisling stopped herself from asking, 'And will you be taking notes?' saying instead, 'I will, bye now, Mammy.'

'Enjoy yourselves. A few hours in the sun will do you both good but be sure to put the sun cream on, Aisling. I won't be able to run you over any E45 cream if you get the sunburn because I've used it all up on Donal's toenail. It's on the mend, by the way.'

'His toenail?'

'No, Aisling, his elbow.'

'Don't be sarky, Mammy, and I'm glad to hear it's getting better.' She hung up as Maureen drew breath to launch into a lengthy account of Donal's health battles with his fungal toenail and followed Quinn in the door of O'Brien's.

Twenty minutes later, clutching a bag containing the two chicken Caesar wraps that promised to be garlicky and delicious, they wandered under Fusiliers Arch into the Green. Quinn led the charge towards the lawn upon which bodies were sprawled in various states of undress, lapping up the good weather.

'How about over there?' he pointed and turned to look at Aisling for confirmation. 'Oh, sorry, I thought you were my wife.' A strange woman gave him a ghost smile and clutched her lunch a little tighter to her chest as she hurried over to the spot he'd pointed out. She commandeered it victoriously.

Quinn frowned, then scanned the area he'd walked across, spying Aisling near the sprinkler waving over. Why was she wiggling about like an eejit, he wondered? She looked like one of those dancing balloon-tube men with an electric fan inflating them that you saw outside car dealerships.

'I'm after getting my heel stuck,' she said when he reached her and planting both her hands on his shoulders, she wrenched her shoe free. 'Thank God for that. I was starting to feel panicky like I was in quicksand.'

Quinn shook his head, and she tiptoed after him to a sun-dappled spot near a flower bed vibrant with pink blooms.

They flopped down onto the soft grass, taking a moment to soak in the surroundings.

'You know we should do this more often,' Aisling said, reaching for the O'Brien's bag.

'Stop and smell the flowers like?'

'Yes,' Aisling nodded. 'We're so busy with the guesthouse and the bistro that sometimes I feel as if we're on one of those running wheels. You know, like Mr Nibbles has in his cage, endlessly chasing around it. We need to just sit and be more.'

'Interesting analogy.' Quinn grinned. 'But I take your point.'

'When we have a baby, we'll have no choice but to slow down.' Aisling had vowed to think positively and chase away any of those niggly negative thoughts before they could take root. 'Sure, look at Moira, she was all; a baby's not going to change my life. And, we know how that worked out.'

Kiera had turned Moira's world upside down in those first few months, but mammy and daughter had settled into a grand routine these days. 'A baby's supposed to change your life. For the better.' She pulled a wrap from the bag and then passed it to Quinn before attacking her own. 'Mmm, this is gorgeous.'

'You've sauce on your chin.' Quinn leaned forward with the serviette from the bag and wiped it off.

A plump duck waddled out from the nearby bushes and sidled over towards Quinn.

'Don't even think about it, Quinn Moran. You know what will happen.'

'Ah, but look at her, poor thing.'

'Poor thing, my arse. The St Stephen's Green ducks are the best fed in the city. She's hardly fading away.'

'I know but she's making me feel guilty. I won't enjoy it if I don't share a little piece with her.' He broke some of the wrap off and tossed it at her. The duck snatched it up and gobbled it down before she began quacking for more.

'See, look what you've done. You've unleashed a monster,' Aisling said. 'Oh, Jaysus!'

Quinn's head swivelled in the direction Aisling's gaze was pinned to and spied a posse of ducks ambling toward them.

'We're outnumbered,' she mumbled through her mouthful. 'I'm not giving them any of mine.' She found herself eating faster.

On Quinn's part, he was experiencing a level of anxiety as the ducks zeroed in on him. One fearless member of the band lunged at his hand, but he held the wrap up out of reach and wriggled closer to Aisling.

'I'll not protect you,' she said. ''Tis your own fault.'

'Ah, Ash, I'm your husband. It's your wifely duty to look after me. I feel like I'm on that tele show, you know the one.'

'When Animal's Attack.'

'Yeah. Ducks don't have teeth do they?'

Aisling glanced at him to check whether he was joking. She couldn't tell.

'I'll toss a little piece over there near yer woman who stole our spot,' Quinn decided, doing just that. There was a flurry of activity, but one duck remained.

'G'won with yer,' Quinn waved his spare hand. 'Shoo, now.'

'Ah, for feck's sake, there'll be none left if I keep this up,'—he busied himself, ripping another bit off, and it all happened very quickly after that. Quinn took fright and dropped the wrap as the duck lunged at him. The duck darted for it, snatching it up with her beak. She waggle-jogged in the direction of the bushes dragging her stolen lunch alongside her.

Aisling erupted into fits at the shock on Quinn's face. 'Ah Jaysus, I'm cryin',' she gasped, thrusting her lunch at him. 'Here, have a bite of mine and know that sharing food is the ultimate show of love where I'm concerned.'

He took it, beginning to see the funny side himself, and it was another few minutes before they'd both got themselves under control.

'If you're not going to have a bite, then I'll have it back,' Aisling said, wiping her eyes and holding her hand out.

Quinn opened his mouth wide and helped himself.

'That was a greedy bite, so it was. Ah, g'won, finish it off.'

Quinn didn't argue, and when he'd balled the sodden wrapper up, he lay down on the grass next to Aisling to gaze up at the blue sky.

She reached over and found his hand, and his fingers snaked through hers. Her tummy ached from laughing, and so did his.

'Do you know the Native American Indians take names from the clouds,' Quinn said.

'That one there looks like a dragon.'

'Where?'

'Over there to the right.'

'No, it looks more like an American hotdog.'

'A hot dog?' Aisling spluttered.

Quinn turned his head toward her. 'Yeah. It's a good job we don't name our kids after shapes we see in the clouds.'

'A good job indeed. Hotdog O'Mara-Moran.'

They both laughed.

'Quinn?'

'Yeah.'

'Everything's going to be okay.'

'Everything's going to be grand, Ash.'

Chapter Five

'You've caught the sun,' Quinn said, landing a kiss on the tip of Aisling's nose as they came to a halt outside the guesthouse. They'd whiled away a blissful two hours in the Green.

'As in Rudolph or sexy sun-kissed?' she asked, noticing he'd got some colour too, only he turned a lovely honey colour straight away, unlike herself.

'Definitely sexy sun-kissed,' he assured her before giving her a wave. Then he was off to the restaurant to get ready for the evening service. Aisling stood with her hand resting on the polished brass knob of O'Mara's front door, watching him saunter off down the street past the rows of old Georgian houses towards Baggot Street. He cut a fine figure with his hands shoved in the pockets of his navy cargo pants, his relaxed gait suggesting he hadn't a care in the world. She was a lucky woman, and she needed to remind herself of that more often she thought, her heart full of love.

As the door was wrenched open, she nearly fell into the guesthouse foyer. Benoit Rosseau, one half of the stylish French couple booked in at the guesthouse for three nights, stood there. He was gushing what sounded like an apology in French. His English was worse than Aisling's French but his wife, Delphine's, was near perfect. Bronagh had developed an instant crush on the glamorous duo proclaiming she loved everything French. As such, she'd pepper them with questions as to their life in Gay Paree each time they appeared in reception.

Moira had called her a fecky Francophile brown noser.

Delphine, Aisling saw looking past Benoit's shoulder, was engaged in animated conversation with their receptionist who was showing her a can of the Arpège scented air freshener Mammy insisted on supplying them with. Given Arpège was what Mammy called her signature fragrance, having the place smelling of her perfume was unnerving. Aisling was forever glancing over her shoulder, thinking her mammy was about to pounce. Her eyes fixed on the French woman. She was fascinating to watch because she spoke with her hands as well as her mouth.

'Aisling, move it.' Moira broke the spell as she made to wheel the pram out the door while their suave French guest held it open for her. 'Jaysus, it's Ronald McDonald's sister,' she muttered, taking in Aisling's sunburnt face.

Aisling would have told her sister to feck off if it weren't for Mr Rosseau because he might not speak English, but some words were universal. So instead, she ignored Moira and made to bend down to say hello to her niece, who was gnawing a Farley's rusk as though her life depended on it.

'No, Aisling. Step away. Don't you dare frighten her with your big red face?' Moira bumped the pram past her sister, who'd flattened herself against the door frame. 'Thanks a million, Mr Rosseau,' Moira tossed back over her shoulder.

Aisling didn't miss the bat of her eyelashes. She didn't blame her either. Benoit Rosseau put her in mind of yer Bryan Ferry man with his casually crumpled suit and that lock of hair he had to push out of his eyes.

He spieled off something in French once more, still holding the door.

Moira and Aisling gazed at him with silly smiles on their faces. He could have said I had potatoes for dinner and made it sound like the promise of sexy things.

His wife called him back over, wanting to show him the air freshener, and Aisling took over holding the door as Moira, now on the pavement, turned back to her sister. 'You'd better hope there's some E45 cream in the cupboard, or you'll peel.'

'Cop yourself on. Just because you're a mammy doesn't mean you have to sound like Mammy.'

Moira's expression was momentarily stricken. 'Jaysus, your right. I did sound like her.' She shook her dark hair, shiny in the afternoon sun. 'I'll be starting conversations with complete strangers next.' Actually, now she thought about it, hadn't she got chatting to a woman in Tesco about the price of nappies being a disgrace only the other day? But, of course, she wouldn't share that with Aisling. 'How'd you get on at the hospital? Was it as bad as you thought it would be?'

'No, not really. I mean, it wasn't fun by any means.'

'No, I'd imagine not.'

They both winced.

'Ah sure, you'll be grand. This one here will have a baby cousin in no time, you'll see,' Moira said, resting her free hand on Aisling's forearm in a gesture of sisterly love.

Aisling decided she wouldn't sit on Moira later after all. She smiled at her. 'Thanks, Moira.'

'And where've you been that has you looking like a baboon's arse?'

'Quinn and I had a picnic in the Green,' she relayed the story of the bold duck.

Moira laughed. 'We're off to meet Mona and Lisa and the babies over in the Green now to feed the ducks, but they'll probably turn their noses up at crusts after dining on O'Brien's finest.'

'Say hello to the girls for me and give the babies a kiss. Bye, bye, Kiera. Aunty Aisling loves you. Yes, she does.'

Kiera dropped the rusk, dribble glistening on her chin. Her eyes, which had turned hazel like her mammy's, opened wide as she took in her aunt's sunburnt face, and her bottom lip began to quiver.

'Told you, you'd frighten her,' Moira said, wheeling her away quickly before Kiera could begin to wail.

Aisling put a hand to her face. It did feel hot. She let the door close behind her, hoping she could slink upstairs to the apartment to hunt out the E45 cream, but Bronagh, seeing her, broke off her conversation with the Rosseaus and beckoned her over.

'Aisling, you're red as a tomato, so yer are. You should know better than to let yourself get burnt like that.' She made a tut-tutting sound, and Delphine voiced her agreement.

'Yes, eet iz very, very bad, Azlin, very, very bad. You, ow you say? Are like the stop traffic light.' She held up her hand in the stop signal.

'She's right, you know. Tis very, very bad. You'll have a face on yer like a raisin by the time you're fifty if you're not careful, my girl. Now, c'mere with you. I'm after telling Delphine and Benoit where they can buy a can of this to take back to Paris with them.' She waved the air freshener. 'Delphine say fragrance for Aisling.'

'Fragwance,' it sounded guttural and exotic at the same time.

'Doesn't she say it lovely, like?'

'Yes, lovely.'

'Delphine and Benoit are after telling me it's true. You know this business of the French drinking wine with every meal.' Bronagh's voice was wonderous.

The couple nodded enthusiastically.

Not entirely true, Aisling thought. They hadn't had a glass of vino with Mrs Flaherty's breakfast this morning.

'And, Delphine's going to share the reason why you never see a fat French woman. Not even when they're going through the menopause.' At this, Bronagh's eyes rounded like saucers.

At the mention of menopause, Benoit sidled over to the display of brochures advertising the delights to be found in Dublin's fair city.

Delphine virtually ate cigarettes; that had to help her weight, Aisling thought, but always up for a hot tip, she moved closer.

The white blooms in the vase on the reception desk would have been a fragrant backdrop behind the angular French woman if reception hadn't reeked of Arpège. Delphine looked from Aisling to Bronagh earnestly.

She reminded Aisling of a picture of Coco Chanel she'd seen in a magazine. Sleek and effortlessly stylish in a little black dress with the sort of hair that would almost twist itself back into a chignon. Her eyes were large and expressive, the colour of black coffee and her makeup, aside from a sweep of statement red lipstick, was minimal.

She was also thin, which, given the heap of bacon, black and white pudding, fried egg and toast she'd got down her that morning along with her boasted wine consumption, didn't seem fair.

Bronagh and Aisling exchanged excited glances. Just the other morning, Bronagh had been lamenting the ravages inflicted on her middle by the menopause. A menopause which, to Aisling's mind, should be recorded in the Guinness Book of Records as the world's longest. Aisling, meanwhile, had wondered out loud to the receptionist as to the weight of hair. For instance, if she cut hers short, not that she had any plans to, but if she did, would that see her shed an instant half a stone? It was an interesting question, one which they'd mulled over while nibbling on custard creams.

'Ladies, us French women, we are passionner about our food.'

'So are us, Irish women,' Bronagh said, and Aisling nodded enthusiastically that this was indeed so.

'We amour soft, ripe cheeses, creamy sauces, decadent desserts, and vino, lots of vino.' She pinched the fingers and thumb of one hand, kissing them and tossing them dramatically away from her lips in a chef's kiss.

'So do we.' Bronagh and Aisling were a duet. Bronagh added, 'And cake, don't forget cake.'

'But,' she wagged a finger with a perfectly oval-shaped nail buffed to a shine, 'we do not overindulge. Non!'

'Non?' Bronagh echoed sadly, and Aisling's shoulders slumped as visions of brie, camembert and tiramisu floated out the door. She should have known there'd be a catch somewhere in there.

'We have only une sliver of the brie or camembert.' She held up one finger and Aisling would have dearly loved to have held her middle finger up back at her. 'A dessert now and again, maybee.' A nonchalant shrug.

'But what about the wine? You have that with every meal,' Bronagh's voice was accusatory.

'Ah, this eez true, but we French women think differently to you Irish women. We eat with elegance.'

Hang on a minute, was she saying Irish women were all pigs at a trough? So what if the guest was always right?

This was taking things too far, Aisling bristled.

'We do not berate ourselves with the thought of diets. Non, non, non. Diet, it eez a dirty word. We eat for amour. We eat with joie de vivre. And, when you eat this way, you do not overindulge. A teeny tiny slice of the cake, understand? It eez enough. It fills your soul. You do not need more because you are happy in your own skin, oui?'

Non. What a load of shite, Aisling thought.

Bronagh was frowning. She ate for love too, the love of cake, only she ate the whole wedge, crumbs left on the plate and all because she was so in love with the stuff.

'But, Delphine, what if you don't have the self-control even if you are full of amour and joie de vivre?' Bronagh asked.

Delphine shook her head. 'Then mon ami, you cannot be French.' Her bony shoulders shrugged once more.

At that moment, both women were prepared to give their Irish nationality up to become French citizens. They'd gladly swear allegiance to the French president if it meant slivers and teeny tiny slices filled them with joy.

They watched in silence as Delphine linked her arm through Benoit's and swept from the guesthouse.

Once the door had closed behind them, Bronagh turned to Aisling. 'Ah sure, it'd be no good being a whippet of a thing like her anyway. Not with the gale force winds in Ireland, you'd spend your days flattened against walls, so.' She opened her drawer and produced the custard creams, holding the packet to Aisling.

'Don't mind if I do, thanks very much.' Aisling crunched into the biscuit sending a spray of crumbs showering down on Bronagh's desk.

'Aisling, eat elegantly, would yer.'

The two women dissolved in laughter.

Chapter Six

Aisling took to the stairs, having filled Bronagh in on her procedure over another two custard creams and, reaching the first-floor landing, she spied Ita lurking in the hallway. A dusting rag was dangling uselessly in one hand, and a can of furniture polish clutched in the other. She'd a startled rabbit expression on her face as she sprang into action. The lid was whipped off the can, and the banister rail overlooking reception sprayed liberally.

At least it wasn't the air freshener, Aisling thought. She was convinced she'd not be able to get the smell of Arpège out of her nostrils for days, thanks to Bronagh's demonstration for the Rosseaus' benefit. Anyone would have thought she was repping the stuff; either that or she was on commission from Mammy.

'I've been flat out, Aisling,' Ita huffed, putting some elbow into it as she buffed up the wooden rail. It was true, sort of. She had been busy, but she worked at her own pace, which couldn't be described as taxing. To her mind, her wages didn't warrant getting herself hot and bothered.

There had been a lot of rooms to make up that day. This was on top of all her usual tasks, including polishing the banisters as she was doing now. 'I've not long finished making up room four, and I'll head upstairs to do room eight after this.' Ita knew the guests in Room 8 were going to be late check-ins. This was why she'd it till last. Ita knew lots of things thanks to the banister rails she kept gleaming because they allowed her to keep up with the comings, goings, and conversations happening in reception. 'That's it then, me done. I'll be away home after that.'

Moira would have asked her if she'd like a medal, but Aisling wasn't Moira who said she was a soft touch.

'Grand, thanks, Ita.' She'd check on the rooms later to ensure there were no chocolate bar wrappers under beds or dust on the bedhead.

'You're face is—'

'Very, very red. Yes, I know. I'm off to hunt down some E45 cream now. I spent too long lazing about on the grass in the Green with Quinn.' Aisling smiled, her face taking on a lazy, dreamy quality. It had been a lovely afternoon, even if she was going to suffer for it now with her sunburn.

Aisling saw the disgruntled flicker on the other girl's face. She clearly thought it was alright for some. It annoyed Aisling, given she hardly made a habit of whiling away her afternoons sun-worshipping. Ita would be an attractive girl with her catlike, green eyes if they didn't have such a sly quality to them, she mused. As for the permanent curl to her top lip, it suggested she felt hard done by. It was off-putting, and indeed, she did walk around with an enormous chip on her shoulder. It made it hard to like her, and there weren't many people Aisling disliked in this world.

'I heard you talking to yer French woman downstairs before.'

'Delphine Rosseau, yes.' Aisling wondered where Ita was headed with this. She'd long suspected their director of housekeeping, as she insisted on being called, skulked about in the corridors of O'Mara's earwigging when she should be working. But Aisling hadn't taken her on, her mammy had. It was back in the days when she was still at the helm. And, while Maureen O'Mara had stepped down, Ita had stayed.

She'd been given the job out of pity more than anything else as a favour to Maureen's old friend Kate Finnegan. Ita had not had an easy time when her parents split up and found it difficult to apply herself at school. She'd left with no qualifications or job, and her mammy was despairing of her. Ita deserved a chance to prove herself, Maureen had insisted. All children did.

Aisling was still waiting for her to prove herself nearly four years down the line. It wasn't as if her mammy even saw much of Kate these days. They were on different paths, she'd said when Aisling had asked after her because while she was loved-up and living in sin with her man friend in a Howth house with a sea view, Kate was in a boxy two-up, two-down over in Phibsborough determined to stay embittered by her divorce. It was sad, really and went a long way towards explaining why Ita was the way she was.

Aisling had been tempted on more than one occasion to give her a written warning, but she didn't like confrontation, and besides, when it came to the staff of O'Mara's, they were family, weren't they? You had to take family as they came, warts and all. It was the way it was.

'I'm not sure about the French.' Ita's eyes narrowed, giving her a snake-like quality as she made this blunt announcement, pausing in her dusting. Her phone began bleeping in the pocket of the cleaning apron she wore over top of her tee shirt and jeans.

No doubt she'd been earwigging while playing that game on her Nokia she was forever at, Aisling thought. She watched her drape the dusting rag over the rail and fumble around in her pocket. Then, finally, she turned the phone off. At least she'd had the grace to redden. Moira's nickname for her of Idle Ita was well deserved. 'Do you know a lot of French people then, Ita?' Aisling tried to keep the sarcasm from her voice but failed. It was hard when Ita had such a supercilious tone.

Ita was oblivious to it. 'No, but my cousin Gillian did an exchange with a French boy last year for a month. Aunt Aine kept asking for his washing, but he never had any to give her. He'd shrug and act like he didn't know what she meant. She couldn't find any piles of dirty clothes in his room either. It was all a mystery that had the whole family pondering what was going on. Then it dawned on her once he'd gone back to France what he was after doing.' She paused for effect.

'What had he done?' Aisling couldn't help her curiosity, but she had a feeling she was going to regret having asked.

'Only worn the same clothes and underpants the entire time he was there.' Ita announced with satisfaction.

Aisling wrinkled her nose. 'But he must have smelled, surely?'

'You couldn't smell anything other than garlic, Aunt Aine said. He reeked of the stuff because he was forever chewing on raw cloves.'

Aisling was right; she did regret having asked. She'd have to watch she didn't find herself sniffing around Benoit when she next saw him. 'Well, erm, thanks for sharing that, Ita. I'll leave you to your dusting, I think.' She planted a foot on the bottom of the stairs, keen to make her getaway.

'Before you go, Aisling, I've something to ask you?'

Aisling waited, her fingers tapping lightly on the banister rail. A pay rise? She wasn't due or deserving, for that matter.

'I'd like to take Friday the fourteenth of September off and Monday the seventeenth, please.'

Aisling did the maths. It was three weeks away. The feeling something else was happening in three weeks niggled at her. 'Are you off on a break somewhere?'

'Yes.'

There was something cagey about Ita's response. It tempted Aisling to probe further even though it was none of her business where she was off to. She was her manager, not her keeper, but she was also her mammy's daughter, and as such, she asked, 'Anywhere nice?'

'Just a few days down south.' Ita's reply was irritatingly vague. 'I know it's the same weekend as Mrs O'Mara's housewarming party, but I'll telephone her and tell her I won't be able to make it.'

Yes, that was why the dates had rung a bell. Perhaps Ita had met a fella and was going away for a romantic weekend with him, Aisling mused. Maybe he'd inject a little joie de vivre into their director of housekeeping! She could live in hope. 'I can't see that being a problem. I'm sure Carmel will be able to fill in that day for you.' Carmel had only been with them a few months, having taken over from Geraldine, their last lady to do the weekend housekeeping shift at O'Mara's. She wasn't far off the pension age and was happy with the hours she'd been given but had told Aisling at her interview she was available to fill in during the week if she was needed.

'I'm not sure about Carmel.'

Jaysus, here we go again! Was she in for a not washing her undergarments tale about Carmel now? From what she'd seen of the older woman, she was a cheerful soul who got more done in the six hours she worked each weekend than Ita did all week. Ita could learn a thing or two from her. Aisling bit down on her lip to stop a retort. She didn't want to rise to the bait.

Ita was undeterred by her manager's steely expression. 'I noticed on Monday that there was a hair in the shower pan of room four, and I found a packet of—'

Enough was enough. 'Ita, you know I check the rooms personally before our guests arrive, and I didn't notice anything amiss.'

'I was only saying. I thought you'd want to know, 'tis all.' Sulkiness washed over her.

'I manage O'Mara's. I'd thank you for remembering that.' Aisling carried on up the stairs, her face feeling even hotter and her heart pounding. It wasn't often she said her piece but needs must, and that had been warranted. 'And, room eight should have been finished at least an hour ago.'

Chapter Seven

Ita scowled at Aisling's retreating figure as she vanished upstairs. Angry tears burned as she returned to her dusting, all the while muttering under her breath about Aisling being an up-herself cow. Who did she think she was? she thought, swiping the dusting cloth over the rail. She hadn't deserved to be spoken to like that. Swipe, swish, swipe. It wasn't fair. She sprayed the can of furniture polish, sending out hundreds of droplets of the lemon-scented cleaning solution.

The O'Mara girls were all the same. They all thought they were something special. It was alright for them with their handsome fellas and mammy, who was all loved-up and happy with her new man. Their daddy hadn't left them by choice either, she thought, and the unpleasant twisting in her stomach tightened as her father's face floated to mind. She shook him away, preferring instead to replay what had unfolded with Aisling. Only this time, she'd a hundred comebacks she'd have liked to have sent her way. She rubbed the rail with her lips moving silently until her arm ached.

The banister's mellow timber glowed, but the shine had gone off Ita's plans. As she mooched off to the cupboard where the housekeeping supplies and trolley were kept, the anger began to seep away too. She hadn't told the truth about having finished Room 4. She'd still got the bathroom to do, and as such, she pulled the trolley out. Ita kept her head down, not wanting to engage with the couple who'd emerged from Room 3 as she trundled down the corridor. The door was partially ajar, and she nudged it open with the trolley, uncaring that it might scratch the timber.

Room 4, a deluxe double, overlooked Iveagh Gardens, and she'd heard Mrs Flaherty blow up this morning about the little red fox. He was partial to visiting the courtyard below under cover of darkness. Aisling called him Mr Fox and Moira referred to him as Foxy Loxy but Ita had her own name for the notorious little fox. Felix. Felix, the fox. It was a grand name, she thought, now abandoning the trolley to move toward the window. Fearless Felix the fox, she whispered, peering down at the courtyard. All the evidence of his raid had been swept up.

Ita admired him for standing up to Mrs Flaherty because the portly cook terrified her. Besides, she insisted on putting the breakfast scraps in the rubbish bin outside. So, she could hardly blame Felix for helping himself. It would be like leaving an open box of chocolates on the reception desk and being surprised when Bronagh helped herself.

Ita had a soft spot for animals. She had a tabby cat with an anxious disposition called Snuffy at home. She was Ita's cat, and no one else's, running away whenever visitors called. The phrase stranger danger could have been invented for her. She'd had her for nearly ten years now, and as an only child, Snuffy was extra special. They'd been through a lot together had she and Snuffy. She volunteered as a cattery assistant for the ISPCA on Saturday afternoons too.

Ita loved her time spent there. It was her job to clean the cat pods and to empty and refill the litter trays. She changed the bedding, and then she got to play with the kittens and cats for a few hours. That was the part she loved. Her mind turned to the older cat who'd been left behind when her family had moved. The full-time staff had called her Deirdre for some unknown reason.

Deirdre loved nothing more than to be brushed. It sent her into seventh heaven, and Ita's arm had ached from all the brushing when she got home last Saturday, much like it did now. She'd have dearly loved to take all the abused, abandoned and neglected furry felines home with her.

There was no chance, though. not with her mam's allergies. She barely tolerated one cat as it was. The feeling was mutual where Snuffy was concerned.

Ita liked to think that she could take all the kittens and cats who needed love home with her when she had her own place. But, when she'd voiced this recently, her mam had said, 'If you don't watch out, Ita. You'll turn into a mad old cat lady.' Ita swallowed down that she'd rather be that than a bitter old divorcée.

There was no time for standing at the window daydreaming though and turning away, she made for the bathroom. Donning the rubber gloves and retrieving the necessary scrubbing brush and spray, she got down on her knees to give it a going over. She'd best do a thorough job because she had the feeling she was on thin ice with Aisling.

The little voice she knew to be her conscience was at her again, telling her she'd no one to blame but herself for Aisling being off with her. She shouldn't have insinuated Carmel wasn't doing a good job. It wasn't fair, and it wasn't true either. Carmel was efficient by all accounts. If Ita were honest with herself, it was the efficiency of O'Mara's newest member of staff that had her rattled.

Ita was many things, but she wasn't silly. She knew she had a tendency to slack off when she thought no one would notice. You could hardly blame her. Cleaning wasn't the most scintillating job. The guidance counsellor she'd been herded off to at school when she'd begun acting out had asked her what her passions were. 'What is it you'd like to do with your life, Ita?' the woman doing her best to look hip and cool, which, given she must be fifty if she was a day was just sad asked. Ita, rebellious to the last, had shrugged as if she hadn't a clue.

She'd known exactly what her passion was though, and what she'd like to do career-wise. The thing was, she'd no intention of sharing that with someone who should know that dressing like a teenager didn't mean you were on the same level as one. Besides, her aspirations had seemed too far out of reach.

She had and still did love singing which was why she'd been a member of a choir for as long as she could remember. She had a strong soulful, mezzo-soprano voice. A voice a choirmaster had once told her was reminiscent of Dusty Springfield. High praise indeed because Ita had adored Dusty Springfield ever since she'd come across an old record of hers tucked away in the stack in the cabinet at home.

The records were a nod to happier days when her mam would turn them up loud, singing along robustly as she did the housework. She'd got her voice from her mammy, who was also a fine pianist. Ita had never had any interest in learning herself, content to sit by her mammy's side on the stool with its turned legs and red velvet cushion. She'd sing while her mam played. She missed hearing her play the old console piano she'd inherited from her father. It was her mam's daddy who'd had the musical gene they'd both inherited.

Not many people knew she could sing. The O'Mara family certainly never asked about what she did with her time outside of work. The sisters had all looked so surprised when she'd got up to sing karaoke at Aisling's hen night, and Maureen had said she hid her light under a bushel.

Singing was something Ita did for the sheer joy of it, not because she wanted to make a career from her voice though. You had to be able to take the knocks and the glory if you wanted to be a professional singer. You were allowed to enjoy the praise, but you had to be able to rise above the criticism too because you could expect plenty of both. Unfortunately, Ita didn't cope well with criticism, and she wasn't resilient. Her father Gerard's face, flickered to mind for the second time that day, and she tried to scrub him away.

She'd left behind the church choir of her youth years ago but had recently begun singing with a choral group once more; the relatively newly formed Gaelic and Raw choir to be precise and it was brilliant. The twenty-strong group was a mixed bag of ages, gender, and backgrounds, all brought together by an advert in the paper and a love of music. They met on Tuesday and Thursday evenings from seven until nine at St Anne's in the draughty old church hall attached to the main building. The hall might have had cracks in the plaster ceiling, and floorboards that groaned with the weight of time, but the acoustics were fabulous. After their Thursday night sessions, a group of them would go for a drink in Madigan's, the nearby pub, before making their way home.

What she loved about G N' Raw, which was their in-house joke and nod to hard rock 80s band Guns N' Roses because of them covering one of their hits, was that instead of dreary old hymns, they sang pop and rock songs. They also sang a selection of Gaelic songs hence their group's name.

It was because of the choir she needed the time off. They were going to be performing in front of an audience for the first time. Gaelic and Raw were part of the planned line-up for the matchmaking festival in the spa town of Lisdoonvarna. The actual festival ran for an entire month each year, and they'd been booked to play throughout a weekend. She got butterflies at the thought of it. Still, Chris, their choirmaster or the Silver Fox as some of the female—and male for that matter—members of the group called him when he was out of earshot, said they were ready. It was all down to him in the first place. He'd an old pal on the festival's planning committee, and he'd sent a recording of them rehearsing. Things had spiralled from there. Oh yes, it was exciting but nerve-wracking at the same time.

What she'd have liked to have done career-wise was veterinary nursing. To achieve that, though, she'd have needed to pay attention and work hard at school, neither of which she'd done. Instead, she'd drifted into this job here at O'Mara's, and while she didn't love it, she didn't hate it either. It was a means to an end until she moved on to bigger and better things. Whatever they might be. It paid her board and lodging in the interim, and there was enough left over for Friday nights out with Molly and Oonagh.

The thing was, she hadn't a clue what she'd do if Aisling decided she'd had enough of her and decided to offer Carmel her job. It was her own insecurity that made her belittle others, and while Ita knew this, her mouth had a life of its own. The unkind words would pop forth as they had with Aisling before. Deep down, she was terrified of not measuring up. If she took the onus off herself and placed it at someone else's door, she hoped she'd continue flying under the radar. It was hard work living your life waiting for a tap on the shoulder and for someone to say, 'I see you for what you really are, Ita Finnegan, and no matter what you do, you'll never be good enough.'

A tear rolled down her cheek and plopped onto the white surface of the shower tray Ita was scrubbing. She sat back on her haunches, wiping it away. Tears wouldn't get her anywhere. Look how many her mam had shed and where had it got her? Nowhere that's where. Looking back, Ita thought that would have been okay if she had decided to get on with her new life like her dad had his. She'd refused to do so though, and as days turned into weeks, then months and now years, she'd grown more entrenched in her bitterness. It was as if she'd forgotten how to be any other way.

Kate Finnegan never missed the chance to slip in comments like, 'Well, of course, things would be different if your father hadn't decided the grass was greener.' Or, 'If it wasn't for that woman, I'd still have a husband, and you'd still have a father.' Her favourite, however, was saved for when she was gazing at the bottom of an empty wine glass. 'I gave that man the best years of my life, and look where it got me?' Ita wanted to scream at her sometimes to stop feeling sorry for herself, but she knew it was pointless because she'd done so once. All it had got her was a wounded stare as her mam asked, 'Haven't I done my best by you, Ita, and that's the thanks I get, is it?'

Self-pity didn't do any good; she knew this, but she couldn't help but feel sorry the girl she'd once been had got lost along the way because she hadn't always been like this. Oh no, as a little girl, she'd brimmed with the confidence of knowing her place in the world. The young Ita had been a kind-hearted, carefree wee soul with a cheery disposition; people had said so.

Alright, she'd turned a bit surly in her teens, but that was normal, wasn't it? Underneath that abrasive teenage skin, she'd still been a happy-go-lucky kid.

Ita wanted to go back to being that girl once more. She wanted to be confident, carefree and cheerful.

She took off her Marigolds, rummaging in her pocket for a tissue with which to give her nose a good blow and recalled the day everything had changed.

Chapter Eight

Dublin, 1993

Ita bowled out of the school gates laughing and squealing at the pelting rain alongside Oonagh and Molly. They were greeted by a cacophonous tooting of horns as parents vied for their respective child's attention in the gloomy afternoon.

'There's Maria, see you tomorrow!' Molly splashed through the puddles towards the shiny BMW idling double-breasted alongside a grey people mover directly outside the school gates. Molly's young Spanish nanny was a law unto herself. She'd be responsible for the newsletter the head would no doubt send home tomorrow. A slap on the hand for the parents' dangerous wet weather parking practices outside school, Ita mused.

Oonagh squeezed her friend's arm, 'My mam's over there. She's waving at you.'

Ita followed the direction Oonagh pointed in, spying Mrs Doyle in her battered Sierra car across the street. She waved back. Mrs Doyle was nice. She always made biscuits whenever Ita or Molly called round.

'We'd give you a lift, but I've got jazz ballet this afternoon. I'll phone you later and tell you how I get on.'

'Good luck!' Ita watched her friend dart across the street before hopefully scanning the rows of cars lining either side of the road. Sometimes her mam, who worked three mornings a week for a small accounting firm in the city, picked her up on wet afternoons. Other times she'd say, 'You won't melt, will you?' Ita sighed, digging her earplugs out of her pocket and jamming them in. She pushed play on her Sony Walkman. The rain was drowned out as 'Uhh Ahh' by Boyz 11 Men blared. She was lucky she still had her Walkman. Sister Mary Catherine had threatened to confiscate it if she brought it with her to school again. At morning break, she'd caught her, Molly, and Oonagh taking turns listening to the compilation tape she'd made the night before.

Her umbrella was in her backpack and, unzipping it, she dug out the plain black pop-up brolly. It was probably a waste of time, she thought as a gust blew icy needles of rain in her face. She doubted she'd make it to the end of the street before the umbrella folded itself inside out. Nevertheless, she popped it open.

She'd choose to get wet over wearing a raincoat any day though. At nearly fourteen, raincoats were not cool, and she'd had a spectacular row with her mammy over this, along with all the other things she insisted on, like the packed lunch with sandwiches. No one had a packed lunch anymore, not unless it came in an actual packet. 'Everybody else buys their lunch, Mam. It's not fair, why can't I?' she'd demanded, watching her mother slap together two slices of bread with a peanut butter filling. On some level, she supposed she should be grateful her lunch was still made for her but right then, she wasn't feeling grateful. Predictably the response to this had been. 'Because we're not made of money, Ita. And I don't care what everybody else is doing. I care what you're doing.' It was so annoying. She wouldn't be surprised if there was a secret Bible of annoying answers to give your teenager that her mam knew inside out.

In the end, Molly had offered to help. She'd asked Mrs Finnegan politely if a list detailing what was okay and what would mean social death for Ita would be of use. Mrs Finnegan had replied that yes she thought it might be. So, Molly had got busy jotting down the dos and don'ts of fitting in at Maryborough College.

Mrs Finnegan had stuck it to the fridge with the magnet she'd brought back from their holiday in Rhodes. Ita fancied she'd seen her mouth twitching at the corners in that way it did when she was trying not to laugh. She hated not being taken seriously.

Some days it was hard being a teenager and getting everything right, she thought, angling the brolly into the wind.

Ita opened her mouth and closed it quickly, catching herself before singing aloud to the chorus. That would not be cool!

The list had helped a little though, she thought, trudging toward home. They didn't argue as much now. Instead, it was her mam and dad who weren't getting on. The closed doors and whispered harsh voices were unnerving. She'd caught snatched words but not enough to make sense of what they were fighting about, and when she'd asked her mam, she'd got very lemony lipped and said nothing.

Ita had confided in Oonagh and Molly that the frosty atmosphere between her parents had her worried, but they weren't much use. Oonagh's dad lived in Birmingham, and she hardly ever saw him. As for Molly's parents, Molly said they spoke to one another as though they were in a courtroom, which given they were both lawyers for a big firm in the city was hardly surprising.

Just as she'd predicted, the umbrella was worse than useless. Ita folded it back down, hoping her sodden state wouldn't mean she'd get earache about how ridiculous it was she wouldn't wear a raincoat. Sometimes she wondered if her mam had ever been young. If she had, then she definitely wouldn't have been cool.

Her pace quickened as she turned onto the quiet street she lived on. Snuffy would be waiting in the hall for her. It never ceased to amaze Ita how the tabby instinctively knew when she'd bowl through the door each afternoon. The blue boot of her mother's hatchback was visible as she neared her house, all but running the last few steps to let herself in the front door. She was soaked through to the skin.

Ita closed the door behind her, half expecting her mam to sing out, 'Close it, Ita, don't slam it.' The house stayed silent though, apart from Snuffy's excited mews.

Ita tossed her school bag down and bent to scoop the cat up. 'Hello there,' she said, rubbing her cheek against the cat's fur. Snuffy wasn't impressed to find her beloved was wet and after an initial purring scrabbled to be put down.

Something was missing Ita thought as she stood dripping on the mat for a moment, trying to work out what it was. There was no light emanating from the kitchen, for one thing, she deduced. For another, there wasn't any hint of what was for dinner wafting down to greet her either. Odd, she thought, calling out. 'Mam, I'm home.'

'In the kitchen, Ita.'

Ita frowned. Her voice sounded funny. She'd best get out of her wet uniform before she investigated what was up though. 'I'll get changed. I'm starving.' She hared up the stairs, Snuffy hot on her heels. The cat bounded onto the bed to keep watch.

It was heaven to clamber out of her damp gear and slip into her snuggly, fleece-lined sweatshirt and tracksuit bottoms. She pulled a thick pair of woolly socks onto her feet too and, pausing to tickle behind Snuffy's ear, padded through to the bathroom.

Ita pulled the towel off the rail and, using it to rub her hair dry, wondered if her mam would let her get highlights in her hair like Molly in time for the school dance. Oonagh planned on asking her mam on the way to her jazz ballet class whether she could do more jobs around the house in exchange for getting blonde foils. She'd ring her after dinner to see how she got on because if Mrs Doyle agreed, then it would be worth her while to sound her mam out with the same idea. She was always saying she should be doing more about the house to pull her weight.

Molly had a new pink baby-doll dress to wear from Miss Selfridge too, but Oonagh and Ita knew new outfits would be pushing their luck on top of the foils so they planned to discuss what they could recycle from their respective wardrobes or perhaps even swap.

'C'mon, let's go see what's for dinner,' she said to Snuffy, retrieving her wet uniform from the floor and retracing her steps down the stairs. The cat padded lightly after her. Odd that the light wasn't on, Ita thought as she walked toward the kitchen. The afternoon was so gloomy it could have been eight pm instead of only getting on for four o'clock in the afternoon.

'Mam, I'll have to put these in the dryer,' she announced as she appeared in the doorway. 'Why are you sitting in the dark?' she asked, seeing her mother at the table. Her hands were clasped around a mug of tea and her gaze fixed on its contents. There was nothing on the cooker either Ita saw glancing over at it, but she could still smell the eggs soft boiled for breakfast that morning. She flipped the light on. 'Mam, has something happened?'

Her mother looked up slowly as if she were coming out of a trance and blinked against the sudden bright light. Ita's throat swelled as panic set in that something serious might have happened. 'What's going on, Mammy? Is Daddy alright?'

'Ita, you'd best sit down.'

Ita didn't want to sit down. If she sat down, then she might hear something she didn't want to. So she stayed where she was, breathing in the wet wool smell of her school sweater.

Her mother sighed and stared unseeingly straight ahead as she tapped the side of her mug with her fingernails. 'Your father's left us, Ita.'

Chapter Nine

Present Day

A plummy British voice outside the room jolted Ita back to the present, and she listened out as she heard a key slide into a door. 'I can't wait to take these sodding shoes off.'

'I don't know why you insisted on wearing them, Sheila. You knew we were going to be doing a lot of walking.'

'Because, Harold, I like these shoes. That's why.'

'But they cripple—'

The voices faded away as the door to the room opposite clicked shut behind the Claibornes who Ita knew were from somewhere on the outskirts of London. Their sons had bought them tickets to Dublin as a fortieth wedding anniversary present. Ita knew this because she'd heard Mrs Claiborne telling Bronagh when they'd checked in. They'd prattled on that the last time they'd been to Dublin had been in the seventies. Harold, or Mr Claiborne, was doing something or other that went over the top of Ita's head at Trinity.

She could take or leave their British guests. The Americans were her favourites. She always went the extra mile for them, placing not one but two chocolates on their pillows because they were generous tippers.

She got to her feet and inspected her handiwork. The bathroom was sparkling. Aisling wouldn't be able to find fault with her cleaning in here, she thought, satisfied. Now, she'd Room 8 to make up and then she could be on her way home to begin putting her plan into action. How would her mam react to her suggestion, she wondered?

Reluctant or enthusiastic, it didn't matter either way because Ita had made her mind up and would not be taking no for an answer.

It was a funny thing, but sometimes she felt their roles had reversed somewhere along the way. Her mammy needed to be taken in hand because it had become crystal clear she'd no intention of helping herself. Oh yes, Ita had high hopes for the long weekend in Lisdoonvarna. She closed the door to the room behind her, trundling back to the supplies cupboard to put the trolley away. The towels and bed linen were kept downstairs, and as she made her way to the ground floor, Bronagh's girlish giggle drifted up to her.

She was chatting away on the telephone, and Ita knew precisely who she was talking to. Mr Walsh. There'd been a time when she'd be giggling and offering her custard creams to any red-blooded male under forty who ventured through the guesthouse door. Not anymore though. These days she only had eyes for Mr Walsh. Bronagh had been a cliched frustrated spinster until she and the dapper gentlemen who had Dublin roots but resided in Liverpool had finally noticed one another.

Was it against the rules to fraternise with the guests, properly fraternise like? Ita wondered not for the first time. If so, then Bronagh had broken them spectacularly when it came to Mr Walsh. He'd been a regular at O'Mara's for years, making the pilgrimage across the sea to visit his sister every year before hooking up with the receptionist. Disgruntlement stirred. There was one rule for Ita and another for the rest of the staff it would seem because Aisling would never snap at any of them the way she had at her.

How was it Aisling, with her hoity-toity ways, had married a good-looking fella like Quinn? She opened the door to the storage cupboard and flipped the switch on. Sure he had the look of Ronan Keating about him. Everybody said so. Then there was Moira, who'd a tongue that could clip a hedge as her mammy would say. Hadn't she bagged herself a doctor no less with a bum you wanted to squeeze? Even airy-fairy Roisin had been given a second chance with that good-looking muso fella of hers.

And while she was on the subject of the O'Mara family, it had broken her heart when Patrick had moved to America. She'd had a crush on the eldest sibling from the moment she'd clapped eyes on him. He was so handsome and self-assured, and he had lovely teeth. But, she pulled a face at the thought of his fiancée, Cindy. That bosom of hers was ridiculous. And she didn't even want to think about Bronagh and Mrs O'Mara being all loved-up at their time of life.

Kiera's pram blocked her path and she muttered, 'Fecking thing,' under her breath, wheeling it out so as she could get down the back of the cupboard for the linen she needed. It wasn't fair, she thought, her bad mood settling over her like a rain cloud and, scooping up the fluffy white towels along with the bedlinen, she breathed in deeply. The smell of the freshly laundered sheets gave the rain cloud a nudge, and she pushed the pram back with one hand before flicking the switch off. The scent was one she enjoyed, unlike that of eggs, she thought, catching a whiff from the kitchen below. It was left over from the breakfast service.

She'd not eaten an egg since that awful day she'd come home from school, and her mammy had announced her dad was gone. The smell turned her stomach.

Bronagh's pealing laughter tinkled out once more, and Ita scowled. No, definitely not fair, she thought, thumping up the two flights of stairs to the third floor.

Room 8 was a superior double room, and her eyes swept the generous space with its plush taupe drapes and matching wallpaper. The carpet, thick under her feet, needed a hoover.

Her gaze took in the array of empty mini-milk cartons and torn sachets of tea and coffee. They were scattered over the tray on which the hot beverage paraphernalia sat. All the remaining sachets had been taken by the guests. As for the bed, the sheets were bunched in a heap as if kicked off. She didn't need to look in the en suite to know every single towel and facecloth would be in a sodden heap on the bathroom floor. Just as the complimentary tea and coffee sachets had gone, so would the travel-sized lotions and potions.

There were three types of guests in Ita's opinion, and she could deduce which of the three had been in any given room by how it was left.

There was the sort for whom a stay in a boutique guesthouse in the capital city was a treat. As such, the room was treated with reverence, and before it was vacated, bedding would be pulled up, wet towels placed in a pile in the bath. A few sachets and smellies would be taken home with them for posterity, and the minibar would be intact. These guests were what Ita called 'the special treaters'.

Then, there were the guests for whom their stay in Dublin was business-related. They'd leave O'Mara's as though in a great hurry. The room would be left in a reasonable state, and they'd not clean out any of the complimentary toiletries or drink sachets. The mini bar, however, was usually depleted. Ita's name for them was 'the workers'.

Lastly, there were her least favourite guests. The grab-everything-they-could guests because they were paying for it. The heating would be cranked, and the room left sauna-like and in disarray. All the sachets would be cleaned out along with the toiletries. Ita had given these guests the name of 'arses'.

The couple who'd vacated Room 8 this morning were arses.

At least they'd opened the curtains. That was something, Ita thought, her nose wrinkling at the source of the greasy, takeaway food smell. The containers were still on the table near the window. She made her way over, heaving the heavy sash window open to allow the balmy breeze outside to blow in and wash away the stale odour.

Cars buzzed up and down the road below, and a sea of people enjoying the good weather milled about in the Green. Ita suddenly yearned to kick off her shoes and feel the grass tickling her bare toes. Reluctantly, she moved away from the view and balled the dirty linen up. The sooner she was finished, the sooner she could be outside enjoying the sunshine. She set about the tasks she could do with her eyes closed, and her mind turned to Gaelic and Raw choir's upcoming trip to Lisdoonvarna.

The matchmaking festival they'd been booked to perform at for the third weekend of festivities in the month-long festival was an institution in Ireland, although Ita didn't know anyone who'd actually, or at least admitted, they'd been. She'd read all about it though when the choirmaster had announced the booking.

The tradition of matchmaking in Ireland was older than the hills, and people had been coming to Lisdoonvarna to make their match forever and a day. People came from all over the world to attend. For one month, the little town in County Clare's the Burren came alive with music and dancing as people sought to make their match and Ita was determined she and her mammy would be there this year to make theirs.

Sure, hadn't she read there was a fella who'd be in attendance who was an official matchmaker. The third generation, no less, and he had a magic book with which he made his matches.

All she had to do now, she thought, tucking the fresh sheets in, was convince her mammy to come with her. Because Ita had a strong belief that if her mammy could find happiness, things would fall into place for herself too. Ita knew she wouldn't be able to spread her wings and find love herself until she'd got her mam sorted, and that was that.

Chapter Ten

‘**A**isling, it's me. Your mammy. I'm on my mobile because I'm at Stephen's Green Mothercare with Moira and the baby Kiera. It's such a lovely day they walked down to meet me. Sure aren't we on a roll with the weather. It's like living in the South of France, so it is.’

She didn't pause to draw breath, continuing to holler into her Nokia mobile phone. ‘We're going to get Kiera sorted with some new babby outfits, and then they're both coming back to Howth with me for lunch. Donal's after taking Moira for another driving lesson. She's sitting her test next week. What was that?’ There was a short pause before she shouted, ‘You're at the doctor's, you say?’

Several heads swivelled towards the smartly dressed, colour coordinated little Irish woman with gleaming chestnut hair, and a cerise silk scarf knotted jauntily around her neck. She'd decided an outing with her youngest daughter warranted dressing up her Mo-pants, although she'd stopped doing the hard sell on the yoga-style pants when she was out and about of late. This was for three reasons.

One being Moira refused to go out with her unless she promised not to accost strangers. She said it was mortifying to watch her mammy demonstrate the versatility of the pants by doing the lunges. The second reason was her supplier. Roisin had been struggling to source enough stretchy, yoga-style pants from the London market stall where she bought them cheap to keep up with demand here in Dublin. However, she'd promised to bring some over with her in a fortnight, and Maureen hoped that would clear the waiting list. Thirdly, her priorities had changed since Kiera was born. It was hard being a successful entrepreneur and a nana. Right now, she'd rather put her energies into the latter.

Moira gave her a sharp nudge with her elbow. 'Stop shouting, Mammy, she can hear you loud and clear.' Jaysus wept. It was mortifying. Worst of all, she only had herself to blame. She was responsible for unleashing this mobile phone monster on the world because it was her who'd taught Mammy how to use it in the first place. The idea was to ONLY use the phone when she looked after Kiera while Moira was at college. It had been a wrench to leave Kiera initially, and she'd needed to know she could get hold of her mammy at all times. Now, she rued the day.

'Your sister's at me, Aisling. It's very distracting, so it is. Listen, ask Maggie to put me on the speakerphone, would you?' Maureen reached over to a nearby rack and stroked a soft green bodysuit.

Moira rocked the pram back and forth in an attempt to keep Kiera interested, given they'd come to a standstill on the edge of the baby department. Why Mammy couldn't have telephoned Aisling while they were in the privacy of her car instead of standing here in the middle of the bustling store, she didn't know, although she'd a sneaking suspicion Mammy liked to show off the fact she had a mobile phone to all and sundry.

Moira side-eyed her, watching as her mammy's mouth opened and closed like a gasping fish that had broken the water's surface for air. She'd a feeling she was going to live to regret having agreed to this outing.

Again it was her own fault. She'd made the mistake of mentioning over the telephone that Kiera was outgrowing everything at a rate of knots and Maureen had suggested a nana, daughter, granddaughter outing to the shops. It had sounded nice in theory, at least. Moira was also hoping that Nana would feel generous, given she and Tom were always strapped for cash. It was the life of the student.

'Quinn Moran,' Maureen seized the chance to get a word in. 'You're to get her to ring me as soon as you know what's what. Do you hear me?'

'The whole fecking store can hear you,' Moira said through gritted teeth.

Maureen stabbed at the off button then held the phone out in front of her, staring at it as though it had mortally offended her. 'He cut me off again. That son-in-law of mine's getting very bossy, Moira.' She shoved her phone back in her handbag. 'Sure, I can remember when Maggie Kinsella was still wet behind the ears from medical school. She wouldn't have minded putting me on the speakerphone so as I could hear the results from the hysterectomy straight from the horse's mouth.'

At the 'h' word, more heads twisted to see who the source was.

'You're not on your mobile now, Mammy, and I'm right here. So turn the volume down.'

Maureen ignored her. There was nothing for it but to wait for Aisling to call her back, so she might as well get on with what she'd come here to do. She plucked the bodysuit off the rack. It had a teddy bear motif on the front and was rather sweet. 'It's the right size, but I wonder if they have it in pink?'

'I like the green,' Moira said. 'There's no rule that says because Kiera's a girl, she must wear pink.'

'There's my rule, Moira. Don't make things complicated for the poor child. Traditions exist for a reason.'

'How is letting her wear different colours complicating matters? She looks well in the green.'

'Take it from someone who's been there and done that.' Maureen tutted determinedly, rifling through the rack of bodysuits for a pink one in the correct size. 'When Roisin came along, your daddy and I were on a tight leash moneywise because we were pouring most of what we earned back into renovating the guesthouse. Babies grow fast, so they do, and Patrick's outfits were like new. It made sense to dress her in those. The blue suited her too, but when she kept getting called Ross instead of Rosi, I had to draw the line. I telephoned your great-aunt Noreen and asked if she'd whip up some babby girl outfits in pink as she's a dab hand with the knitting needles and sewing machine. Lo and behold, a few weeks later, I'd enough pink outfits to do all three of you. It was a good thing really because when Aisling was born, she looked like yer Kojak wan until her hair grew.'

Moira shook her head, and her ponytail swished like a horse's tail. 'Mammy, no one will mistake Kiera for a boy if she's wearing green. She's far too pretty for one thing.' She could say things like that because she was her mammy after all.

'Be that as it may, Moira, and far be it for me to argue, I'm only your mammy after all, but if people start calling her Keagan or the like, it's on your head.'

Moira draped the all-in-one on the roof of her pram feeling triumphant as she wheeled it into the heart of Dublin's 3 to 9-month-old summer baby fashions.

The pram was soon laden with tee shirts and leggings, romper suits, sleepsuits and bodysuits in yellows, greens and the odd pink to pacify her mammy. Moira steered clear of anything with blue in it because she wasn't able for another lecture from Mammy.

'I can't believe how many gifts of size 0-3 month outfits we were given when Kiera was born.' Moira lamented, plucking at a plain, white cotton dress before deciding it wasn't practical. 'Sure, I've enough clothes to keep Dublin's newborn babies dressed stylishly for a year and not a single thing to fit one bonny five-month-old.'

That's when Maureen's eyes lit up, and their shopping trip swiftly turned pear-shaped.

Moira watched in horror as she elbowed a fellow nana shopper out the way. A young mum whose baby, mercifully, was in the pram, not her arms was next, and then she snatched up a pink dress. It had more frills than she'd had hot dinners. Maureen was further delighted by the discovery of matching knickers and bonnet.

Moira looked on horrified as her mammy held it up and flapped it at a woman with an enormous belly. A matador to the bull. The woman was futilely trying to shrink into the rack of vests she was standing beside as Maureen exclaimed that her granddaughter, the baby Kiera, would look a picture in it.

'No, Mammy. Put it back,' Moira finally found her voice. 'She'll look like a traveller baby off to one of their gypsy wedding extravaganzas in that.' She made her way over to her mammy, attempting to wrestle the baby girl monstrosity off her, but Maureen was having none of it. Her grip on the coat hanger was vicelike.

'She'll look like a baby girl whose nana loves her in it, so she will,' she hissed back at her daughter.

A tug-of-war ensued.

'Excuse me. Is there some sort of problem? We do have more stock out the back, ladies so there's no need to tussle over it.' Claire Dornan the customer service manager of the Stephen's Green's Shopping Centre branch of Mothercare, had seen showdowns like this before, but it was usually over a sale item. She'd been alerted to the kerfuffle by a young mother indignant at nearly having been knocked down by a bolshie, short woman with a cerise scarf knotted about her neck.

'Claire, is it?' Maureen squinted at her name badge, not loosening her grip on the hanger.

Claire nodded. There was a gleam in yer woman's eyes that said she meant business. Perhaps she should have alerted security.

'I'm Maureen O'Mara, and I'm sure you'll understand my plight here, Claire. Grandchildren are gifts of God, are they not?'

Claire Dornan nodded, 'They are indeed.'

Satisfied, Maureen continued, 'Grandchildren are His way of compensating us for growing older. All I want is the chance to show off the baby Kiera there in the pram, in this beautiful wee dress. It's not a lot to ask now, is it, Claire?'

Moira's eyes narrowed. She didn't like this being on a first-name basis with yer Mothercare wan.

Claire looked from mother to daughter. Maureen might be slightly shorter, but she'd a more intimidating air than yer Demi Moore lookalike wan. It was survival of the fittest in this world. Accordingly, Claire bobbed her head, showing off a strip of regrowth to rival Bronagh's zebra stripe as she agreed wholeheartedly with the little woman's sentiment. She laid it on thick, gushing about how delightful Kiera would look in the pink dress with the layers and layers of frills. And sure, she added, risking a glance at Moira, wasn't she a lucky little babby to have a nana who wanted to buy her such a bonny outfit to wear?

Moira called Claire a fecky brown noser, customer service woman under her breath, shooting daggers at her and Mammy as she all but linked arms with Claire and skipped toward the counter. Then, remembering she wanted Mammy to pay for the clothes draped on top of the pram, she hurried after them.

Ten minutes later, they were in the car park loading the boot of the car with Mothercare bags.

'I can't believe you invited yer Claire wan to the housewarming party.' Moira said, unbuckling Kiera from the pram.

'And why wouldn't I? Sure, she was a lovely girl. I'm delighted she's free.'

'Girl's a stretch. She's fifty if she's a day.'

They bickered over the dress and Maureen's habit of inviting random people to the housewarming all the way to Howth. It was only as the sparkling waters of the harbour came into view that the choppy seas inside the car were calmed.

Maureen promised on Patrick's life to keep the dress at her house and that she'd only ever pop Kiera in it when Moira wasn't present. She also said she'd stop asking people she barely knew to the party. But only on the condition that Moira promised not to tell Donal she was after doing it again in the Mothercare.

A truce was reached.

The intimate welcome to Mornington Mews Maureen had initially planned had swelled into the Howth house party of the year. The stress of the impending party wouldn't do Donal's toenail any good at all, and she wanted it cleared up before the event. She shuddered at what the neighbours would think otherwise, and she was desperate to get friendly with Amanda and Terence next door. They were precisely the right sort of people to mix and mingle with when you had a house with a sea view.

Chapter Eleven

'Stay still for Mammy, Kiera, and we'll have you changed in no time,' Moira dictated as Kiera promptly attempted another roll. She was lying on her changing mat on the floor of her nana's living room bathed in a puddle of sunshine. It wasn't the only puddle she was lying in, Moira thought, swiping the wet nappy out from under her and folding it up.

'You were the same,' Maureen said as she watched her daughter go into battle with a fresh nappy. 'Always on the go, so you were. That's why you want to get her name down for the Irish dancing lessons, Moira. You need to channel her energy and focus her talent.'

'Mammy,'—Moira blew the hair that had slipped from her ponytail out of her face as she huffed—'she's not a future star on the Russian gymnast circuit, and she isn't even six months old yet. We don't even know if she has any talent.' Moira held her daughter by the ankles and lifted her so as she could slide the nappy under her.

'She's my granddaughter. She has oodles of talent, and I'm not talking about gymnastics. I'm talking about Irish dancing. I don't know, Moira,'—Maureen shook her head, and her hair, freshly coloured its current chestnut just the other day, swished back and forth—'when were you last after having your ears checked?'

'For feck's sake,' Moira muttered, getting het up as Kiera managed to flip onto her side before she could wrest the nappy into place. 'She's leaning more towards being a Houdini escape artist than a Flaherty protégé twinkletoes.'

'Determined is what she is, like her mammy. It will stand her in good stead, so it will. Mark my words. And that's another thing, Moira. You're a mammy now, and that means you're going to have to curb that mouth of yours because children are parrots, so they are. Your father was a good one for the fecking this and that's until I put a stop to it. I had to have a stern word with him after what happened.'

Moira couldn't remember her beloved daddy ever using bad language. However, she had once seen him do a rude finger sign behind Mammy's back. Unbelievably her mammy had somehow known what he was up to, snapping, 'And don't think I don't know what you're after doing with that finger of yours, Brian O'Mara.'

A teenage Aisling had whispered to her wide-eyed little sister, 'See, I told you she has eyes in the back of her head.'

'What happened?' Moira asked, feeling victorious as she stuck the tags down firmly on either side of Kiera's hips. 'There, done.'

'You happened, that's what. You told yer poor woman on the till in Boots to feck off away with herself when you were three. Three, Moira! Out of the mouths of babes. Mortified, I was. It was the soap for you when I got you home, I don't mind telling yer. I had to walk miles out of my way whenever I needed the E-45 cream for years after that, and I felt like I'd a sign hanging above my head for all to see.'

'Saying what?' Moira sat back on her heels, eyeing her mammy, who was getting pink in the face at the retelling of her tale.

'Saying, there she goes, yer woman who's the mammy of that foul-mouthed, dark-haired little girl who looks like butter wouldn't melt.'

'Ah, well now, Mammy, yer Boots woman must have upset me.'

'She asked you whether you were having a lovely day out with your mammy, so.'

She didn't have a good track record when it came to Boots, Moira thought. The incident at the pharmacy with Andrea that had seen them collared for shoplifting a pregnancy test sprang to mind. It had been a misunderstanding, of course, but she still shuddered whenever she ventured past the chemist shop.

'I can't believe I've only just remembered,' Maureen tapped her forehead.

Moira began packing away the changing supplies. 'Remembered what?'

'I'm after having had a vision,' Maureen announced.

Jaysus wept, Moira thought, dropping the balled up wet nappy into a nappy bag. She was in the presence of the oracle. She was almost afraid to ask. 'What sorta vision?'

'I was wearing a sarong—'

'If it's going to be rude, I don't want to hear it.'

'Don't you be cutting me off and all, young lady. I was wearing a sarong wrapped around my waist, and I'd my swimsuit on. You know the one-piece I took to Los Angeles with the special ruching for the tummy control? And I'd a red hibiscus flower behind my ear and a lei around my neck. Donal was strumming a ukulele, and that's when I woke up and knew Him up there had sent me a sign.'

'A sign for what? Discount flights to Honolulu?'

'No. A theme for the housewarming party.'

'I still think my idea was a good one.'

'No, Moira, it wasn't. It's been done a thousand times before. We shan't be having a Superheroes party. We need something new and exciting, and I've just the ticket now after my epiphany.'

Moira pulled a face. She'd fancied dressing up as Wonder Woman and lassoing Tom. That would have been something new and exciting.

'We'll be having a Hawaiian themed luau.'

Moira eyed her mammy speculatively for a moment picturing herself in her bikini sipping cocktails because that's what people did in Hawaii. 'I like it. I can wear my bikini and yer leis thingamabob.'

'No, you cannot. You're a mammy now, for one thing, Moira. It's the full swimsuit you'll be wearing from here on in. Your days of the wispy bits of string are gone.' She thought for a moment. 'Actually, you're not to be wearing any sorta swimsuit to the party unless it's covered by a sarong.' The last thing she wanted was her three girls swanning around like they should be working for yer Hugh

Hefner wan in his Playdough Mansion. Not when she wanted to make a good impression on Amanda and Terence next door. 'Do you see a swimming pool out there?' She waved her hand toward the strip of lawn, which gave way to her pride and joy, her sea view. 'No, you don't.'

All Moira could see was a disgruntled poodle. He wasn't allowed back in the house until he'd done his business. He'd been letting off something terrible when they'd returned from the shops, and Maureen had herded him out the French doors. 'I can so still wear a bikini. I've very elastic skin, and it's bounced back to where it's supposed to, for your information.' Next, she'd be telling her she needed to wear the lady pads when she exercised. She might need them when she laughed but so far, so good when it came to the walking, which was the only type of exercise Moira did apart from the riding.

'I wasn't talking about your tummy. I meant you can't make a holy show of yourself with your bits hanging out now you're a mammy. How do you think the baby Kiera will feel looking back on photographs when she's older? She'll turn the page to be confronted with her mammy prancing about wearing nothing but a few pieces of dental floss. So put yourself in the poor babby's shoes, Moira.'

'She doesn't wear shoes.'

'Don't get smart. How would you have felt if I'd gotten around in an itsy-bitsy bikini every chance I got when you were a child?'

'Sick.'

Donal breezed in at that moment, a welcome distraction from their topic of conversation.

'How're you there, ladies?' he beamed, striding barefoot through the open-plan living and dining area. 'And how's my little princess today? Come and say hello to Poppy D.'

Kiera gurgled and grinned gummily up at her poppy. Her plump arms waved about.

'Bend at the knees, Donal,' Maureen instructed as he made to pick Kiera up. 'We don't want you putting your back out on top of the toe. How was your morning tea with Anna?'

Donal did as he was told, and once he'd scooped up Kiera, he answered, 'Grand. I think she's got a fella on the go. She's wearing her hair in a new style. Suits her it does, and she'd a twinkle in her eye and a bounce in her step. It was good to see. She works too hard, that girl. It's about time she had some fun too.' Anna, who worked as an emergency room physician, lived and breathed her job.

'Well, be sure to tell her to bring her young man to the housewarming party. I'm after telling Moira about my vision last night.' Maureen had woken Donal to share her dream with him at three am. He was all for a Hawaiian themed party if it meant he could pay a visit to that new Outdoor Scene store and buy a barbeque. A big one. He'd always wanted a barbeque with all the bells and whistles. So while Maureen had eventually dropped off back to sleep to dream she was dancing the hula, Donal had dreamt he was barbequing up a storm.

Moira wasn't listening. Her gaze had gone straight to his foot. She didn't want to look at his big toe, but she couldn't help herself and, feeling like a voyeur passing the scene of an accident, her eyes slid towards it. Oh, sweet Jaysus! How was she supposed to concentrate on her driving lesson knowing that thing was only inches away from her? She'd have the theme tune from Jaws playing in her head each time it edged nearer. And she'd her test next week. It wasn't good.

Donal jiggled Kiera about, making her giggle, before asking Moira, 'And what news do you bring with yer today, young lady?'

Moira decided she'd have to cast Donal's big toenail from her mind. There was nothing else for it. It took a concerted effort on her part, but she filled him in on Aisling and Quinn's trip to the doctors. 'They're after getting the results of the test they had done at St James's.' Her eyes felt the magnet pull toward the toenail, and to distract herself, she told him about her and Maureen's outing to Mothercare.

Maureen had insisted on retrieving the dress that had caused all the angst, and Donal wisely agreed that Kiera would look pretty as a picture in it.

Moira scowled but was mollified when he added, 'Mind, she looks pretty as a picture in whatever you put her in, Moira.' He turned back to Maureen. 'Aisling and Quinn will be grand. They'll be a proud mammy and daddy before they know it. And you'll have a little babby cousin to play with, so you will.' He jiggled Kiera.

'Ah-hem, Donal.' Maureen cleared her throat. 'I think the baby Kiera wants her nana. She'll be due to have her bottle soon and a nap, won't she, Moira?'

Kiera was happy where she was with her poppy.

'Ah no, she's grand, Maureen. Aren't you, princess?' He jiggled her again.

Moira laughed, feeling a warm glow spread through her at the delight on her daughter's face. Her fine hair stood up in dark tufts, and her eyes were more hazel than brown and already full of mischief. Her cheeks were two pink spots in a chubby face seemingly always decorated with lipstick marks from either her mammy, her aunty Ash, Bronagh, or her nana. At five months, she'd doubled her birth weight and had taken to solids like a duck to water, although she still enjoyed her bottle before naps. She could sit up with support now and was already beginning to push up onto her elbows when lying on her stomach. Her favourite trick was pushing whatever was on the tray of her high chair onto the floor to see who'd come running to pick it up for her so she could do it all over again.

Moira had her in a grand routine these days too, which she made sure her mammy and Tom's mammy Sylvia stuck to like glue. The two nanas had exchanged amused glances when they'd been handed a carefully typed sheet informing them of what was to happen when. They'd both refrained from mentioning that between them, they'd raised eight children of their own. The Wednesday Nina had looked after Kiera had been filled by Moira's new friend, Mona. She was glad of the extra spends and said her daughter Tallulah loved the company.

Best of all, Kiera had begun to sleep through. Moira felt like she'd rejoined the human race and was enjoying being back at college, where she was studying for her fine arts degree. Tom was no longer operating in zombie mode either as he split his time between his two girls, waiting at Quinn's, medical school, and studying.

'Moira? Are your ears painted on?'

'What? Oh, bottle. Yes. I'll make it up soon. Weren't you going to make sandwiches for lunch? I'm starving.'

'Three cheese and piccalilli coming right up.'

Maureen beamed as she padded off to the kitchen. There'd be plenty of time for holding Kiera once she'd waved Moira and Donal off on their driving lesson. Plenty of time to pop her granddaughter into her new dress. She'd show off how sweet she looked by taking her for a stroll around the shops in Howth. She might even telephone Rosemary and see if she was free to meet for a coffee.

At the thought of Rosemary, she frowned. Their friendship had been strained of late as the judging date for the Howth Hand Quilter's Association annual competition drew nearer. It was only a month away now, and Rosemary had behaved furtively by refusing to let her see her entry into the Memories section. She was terribly competitive was Rosemary, and they were both chasing gold with their quilts.

Maureen knew her friend's daughter Fenella had honeymooned in Hawaii. You'd have thought Rosemary was right there with the happy couple in Waikiki the way she'd gone on and on about the rose petals and chocolates scattered on the bed. Not to mention the view of the beach from the honeymooner's suite. She could put up with hearing all about Fenella's five-star week in Waikiki for the millionth time if it meant finding out about the sort of things you ate at a luau. Maureen wanted the theme to feel authentic. It would smooth things over between her and Rosemary too.

'Can Pooh come back in?' Moira called over. 'He keeps giving me that Lassie Come Home look of his.'

'Don't be fooled,' Donal said.

'I thought he was warming to you?'

'He is,' Maureen chirped before Donal could reply. 'Sure, he's stopped the piddling in the wellington boots. If that's not progress, I don't know what is. If Donal were to start to refer to himself as Daddy, that might help him bond with

Pooh too. And yes, he can come in but tell him if he starts with his windy tricks again, he'll be straight back outside again, no messing.' She opened the bread bin and retrieved a loaf before hunting down the spread and piccalilli. 'I'm feeling aggrieved with that vet of his, so I am. This special diet he put Pooh on, which, by the way, is costing an arm and a leg, was supposed to help settle that side of things down, but he's as bad as ever. I was mortified when he let off while Amanda from next door was here for coffee the other morning. I'm sure she thought it was me.'

Moira sniggered and got up to let the poodle, who was a law unto himself, back inside.

'Oh, Donal, I forgot to mention I dropped a spare key next door in case we ever manage to lock ourselves out.'

'Smart thinking, Maureen.'

Maureen began slapping together the sandwiches, slathering Donal's favourite chutney on the bread nice and thick for him the way he liked it. She didn't bother mentioning Terence's odd response when he'd opened the door to her yesterday. She'd dangled the key on the pineapple key chain she'd found in the odds and sods drawer in front of him. 'Terence, would you mind holding on to this for us in case we ever get locked out?'

Terence had given her a peculiar smile. If she hadn't known better, she'd have said it was predatory.

'I did wonder, Maureen,' he said, taking the keyring from her.

'Wonder what?' she'd asked.

But he'd simply winked and jiggled the pineapple on the keychain.

Perhaps he was after having a funny turn. It was best to leave him to it, Maureen decided.

Now, she pushed Terence's strange reaction yesterday aside to glare at the telephone. It remained silent the way it always did when you were waiting for an important phone call. She'd give it another half an hour, and if she'd not heard from Aisling by then, she'd chase her down. Her stomach tied itself in a knot that would have made the Girl Guiding movement proud. It was hard sitting on the sidelines watching her daughter's heart slowly breaking a little more with each month passing her and Quinn by with no sign of them being blessed.

Nobody bothered to tell you when you had your babies that you never stopped worrying about them, she thought with a glance at Kiera. She was still enthralled with her poppa D's antics. There was no cut-off point where you gave yourself a pat on the back and thought, there now I've done my best, my job is done, off into the world you go.

Her eyes moved over to Moira. Some things though you had to find out for yourself, she thought, calling her and Donal to the table.

Chapter Twelve

M aureen sat at the table, clicking the ballpoint pen on
and off as she stared into space. Her party planner
notebook was open in front of her, and she'd written the
word 'Menu' on a new page. She'd even gone so far as to
underline it twice, but apart from cheese and pineapple
sticks which were so passé these days, she couldn't think
of a single thing to write down.

What did people eat at a Hawaiian luau?

There was so much to organise and she wasn't sure
where to start. Donal was all for throwing sausages on the
new barbeque he was on about getting. Sure, what was
wrong with a tasty pork sausage slapped between a slice
of buttered bread? he'd asked.

Maureen had silenced him with a look. Their fellow
Mornington Mews residents, Amanda and Terence and yer
Barbie and Ken wans were not sausage-in-bread sorta
people.

Maureen had conceded, however, that an events
manager might be taking things a tad far as she'd clinked
glasses with Donal. They'd been lapping up the late
afternoon sun in the garden enjoying crackers and cheese
along with a glass of wine. That was what you did after all
when you had a sea view. They'd smiled at one another
fondly as they'd agreed there'd be no sausages and bread
and no events manager but that there'd be ukulele music.
Donal had gone so far as to volunteer, Niall from The
Gamblers services. The foundation of any successful
relationship was compromise they'd thought smugly.

Maureen decided it wasn't the time to broach the ever-expanding guest list.

The Gamblers would play a few numbers too because an evening of nothing but the ukulele music would make you want to pull your hair out. The Kenny Rogers tribute band, with her Donal as the main attraction, always got people dancing, and a party wasn't a party without dancing.

They could have lanterns strewn about the garden, she thought, now tapping the page in front of her, and giant colourful paper blooms. She could get the girls to help her make those. Which one of them was it had gone through an origami phase? Probably Rosi, she decided. Origami sounded like a Rosi sorta thing. Sure, it would be a party that would have everybody talking for months to come. Then, come winter, when they were miserable in the rain, all they'd have to do was think of the great luau party Maureen and Donal had thrown to be smiling again.

The empty page winked up at her. The library was a good starting point for a suitable cookbook, and failing that, she'd have to hope Rosemary's daughter Fenella proved helpful. There were phone calls to be made too. She needed to give all those on her invitation list who'd had the good manners to RSVP a bell to tell them she'd decided the party was going to have a theme. A thought occurred to her. Should she mention appropriate attire was to be worn? She was no prude, but the last thing she wanted was Bold Brenda flouncing in wearing her skirted bathing suit. Or Randy Rory from the yacht club squeezed into the underpants that were supposed to be swimming trunks. Pretty sundresses, sarongs, shorts, and flowery shirts were more what she had in mind.

A vision of herself standing in the doorway, meeting and greeting her guests with colourful leis to drape around their necks flitted to mind. It was shoved aside, however, by yet another question springing to mind. To hula dance or not to hula dance? She turned the page of the notebook and wrote a new heading, 'Who will dance the hula?' Maureen didn't know much about the hula dancing but imagined there'd be a lot of hip action, and she didn't know if hers were up to the job. She'd have to ring around some of those private entertainment companies.

Pooh gave an excited yelp in his sleep. He was curled up at her feet, and she glanced down to see his nose twitch. The sight made her smile fondly at him, but her expression morphed into a frown as the burbling coming from the guest bedroom where the travel cot was set up began to change in pitch. Kiera was making it known she was fed up with being in the cot.

Maureen glanced at the wall clock in the kitchen. It had been a good twenty minutes since she'd laid her down for her nap after they'd waved her mammy and Poppy D off. They were going to be gone a few hours as this was the last practice Moira would squeeze in before her test. Kiera had obviously decided she didn't want a nap today, she thought with a sigh because it was clear she wasn't going to settle. It was no good sitting here trying to conjure up party food ideas. She couldn't concentrate, not knowing her precious granddaughter would begin wailing any minute.

She marched into the darkened room, pausing to pull open the curtains. The room was instantly awash in a sunny early afternoon glow.

'You've got your nana wrapped around your little finger, so you have,' she said as she plucked up the glassy-eyed five-month-old who beamed deliriously at the sight of her. Maureen's heart softened as it did every time she laid eyes on her granddaughter. 'You are too gorgeous for your own good. That's the problem.' Maureen planted a kiss on her soft, warm cheek before announcing, 'Right then, madam. You and I will try and get a hold of your aunty Aisling to see how she fared at the doctors, and then we are going to pop you in your new dress and go for a walk. We won't waste this glorious afternoon by sitting about. We'll show you off, so we will. You'll be the bonniest babby in Howth. All of Ireland, for that matter. What do you think of that then?'

Kiera gave her nana a gummy smile which told her she thought it a grand idea.

At the word 'walk', Pooh rose from the dead and began yapping while Kiera made a grab for her nana's scarf.

A few minutes later, Pooh had been quietened by an extra scoop of his special doggy biscuits and Maureen was perched on the sofa. Kiera was nestled back on the cushions alongside her, happily rattling her linking rings. She gazed at the phone in her hand for a moment, trying to decide what number to ring first to track Aisling down. She was loath to ring her mobile because Quinn kept giving her short shrift, and it wasn't good for son-in-law relations.

Fifteen minutes later, she was staring at the phone once more, but this time she was perplexed. Nor was she any wiser as to the outcome of Quinn and Aisling's doctor's appointment. The pair of them had done a disappearing act. 'Who do they think they are, Kiera? Yer international man and woman of mystery?' They weren't answering their mobile phones either. It was all a worry, and there was nothing for it but to wait for Aisling to telephone her when she was ready. Maureen hoped it wasn't bad news they were after being told but, if it was, she'd be there to pick up the pieces and get them back on track. They all would. At least she'd touched base with Bronagh as to whether Leonard would be coming to the party. That was something.

Bronagh had informed her Leonard would be delighted to attend before telling her a Hawaiian party was sure to be great craic for them all. She hoped she was joking about wearing a coconut shell bra. You could never tell with Bronagh. It had been satisfying to put a fat red tick next to Leonard's name.

She hadn't mentioned the party's theme to Rosemary when she'd rung to see if she was free for coffee that afternoon. She'd wait and talk to her in person, she'd decided as Rosemary informed her that her telephone call was good timing. She informed Maureen that she had a pair of boots suitable for rambling put away for her at the specialist shoe shop run by yer man who looked like a leprechaun. At this point in the conversation, Maureen had interrupted to say she wasn't familiar with any specialist shoe shop run by a leprechaun. Rosemary had elaborated by saying if you blinked, you'd miss it, tucked in as it was down the little laneway only the locals seemed to know about.

'Oh, you mean the shoe shop run by yer man who looks like an elf. I'm with you now,' Maureen had replied.

'That is neither here nor there, Maureen, given the original word for leprechaun was derived from the Irish leath bhrogan, which meant shoemaker.'

Maureen rolled her eyes. Rosemary could be such a know-it-all at times.

Once they were on the same page, Rosemary informed Maureen she was after her opinion about the boots because they were an extortionate price for a widowed woman on a pension.

Maureen said she'd be delighted to give Rosemary a second opinion. In another life, she'd have been one of those mystery shoppers. And very good at it, she would have been too.

Rosemary hadn't seen the relevance of this. All she wanted was Maureen's honest opinion as to whether yer leprechaun man was trying to fill his pot with more gold at her expense.

However, they'd decided not to debate the point and had arranged to meet at the café run by yer man who looked like a pirate in forty minutes. They'd check out the shoes after they'd put the world to rights.

Maureen faffed about sliding the frilly knickers over Kiera's fresh nappy before popping her into her new dress. The finishing touch was the bonnet, and she secured the ribbon in a big bow beneath her chin. Satisfied, she got up, ignoring the creaking of her knees as she took a step back to admire the overall effect. 'What was your mammy on about? You're a picture, so you are, Kiera.' Her granddaughter's round face peered up from beneath the white frill, and Maureen announced she had to fetch the camera. 'So we can show yer silly mammy how pretty you look. She never did have much fashion sense that one.'

She left Kiera fascinated by a shifting pool of sunlight on the carpet. She scuttled off to hunt the camera down, hoping it had a film in it. Donal had been camera happy when the deep pink snapdragons he'd planted in spring had reached their full glory last week. She located the camera on top of the fridge and thanked Him up there, seeing two shots left.

'Kiera, look at the camera for Nana and say cheese,' she said, having moved her granddaughter so as the sun wasn't behind her. The sofa provided a stormy backdrop to the little girl's pink outfit. Her finger pressed the shutter as Pooh slunk into the frame, his arse captured on Kodak for posterity.

Maureen muttered under her breath before dragging him out the way. She'd only one shot, and in a no-nonsense tone, told him to 'sit'. It was her own fault, she supposed, for having taken so many pictures of him when he'd first come to live with her. Every time he saw the camera, he struck a pose.

'Right, Kiera, one, two, three.' This time she got the money shot.

She really was a wee dote. It wasn't only her who thought so either. Kiera won hearts wherever she went. She'd have to mention to Moira entering her in the Rose of Tralee competition as soon as she was old enough. She'd win the crown, hands down. Sure, that would be a feather in the O'Mara family's cap, so it would. Hang on a minute, though, she thought, rewinding the film; could non-Kerry residents enter? She pondered this as she waited to retrieve the canister from the back of the camera. Sure, hadn't they had a grand holiday in County Kerry when the children were still all at home? If she mentioned that, Kiera was bound to be given a special exemption, she decided, taking the roll of film out and dropping it in her bag. It could be left at the pharmacy while she was in the village.

All that was left to do was put on her lipstick, and they'd be on their way. She'd need a new one of those too while she was at the chemist, she thought, using her little finger to gauge out what was left of her favourite coral summer shade. Then, arranging Kiera in her pram and fetching Pooh's lead, she plonked her sun hat on her head and the trio set forth for Howth. It was a pity Amanda was nowhere to be seen, she thought, rattling over the length of the curved pebbled driveway, Pooh prancing along beside them. She'd have liked to have shown Kiera off in her new dress and bonnet. Still and all, it was a glorious day and that was something to be grateful for indeed.

Chapter Thirteen

Maureen waited for a break in the pootling traffic, her eye having been caught by the floaty summer dress in the window of her favourite Howth boutique. It was red with white flowers on it, and all thoughts of the sarong she'd planned on wearing to the party went out the window. That dress over there would be perfect for the party. It was even in the wrap style!

Young Ciara, the waif who managed the shop, had recommended this style to her as flattering for women who'd reached a certain age and borne children. Four of them, in fact, Maureen was always quick to inform her. All with pumpkin heads on them.

She liked to call in when she was out and about with the babby Kiera although Maureen had been quick to point out she was Kiera with a 'K'. She didn't want Ciara getting notions about namesakes. They weren't on that sorta basis. There was no time to call in now, though, she saw with a quick glance at her watch.

A red sports car with the top down slowed, and the driver, a woman with a scarf knotted over her head and dark sunglasses covering her eyes, waved out for Maureen to cross. Checking the other lane was clear she herded the pram and Pooh across the road, calling out a thanks a million to the courteous woman who took off with a roar.

There was something to be said for a red sports car, Maureen always thought. It spoke of glamour and an exotic lifestyle. She gazed after it clocking the number plate, 'Hot Stuff.' Mind, drowned rat was probably more applicable given Ireland's rainfall. Still and all, as she mounted the pavement with the pram, she paused to imagine herself and Donal whizzing about on a day like today with the wind in their hair. No, she decided to put the notion aside. Aside from the rain, there was the wind, not to mention the babby Kiera. It wouldn't be at all practical. Sure, one good gust, and she'd lose her bonnet.

Ah, here was Rosemary now, she saw, waving out at her friend who was thunking down the pavement with her hiking pole. She looked as though she was off to tackle the Matterhorn instead of meeting a pal for coffee. Maureen gave a sharp intake of breath as the pole nearly skewered an elderly gent when Rosemary raised it towards her in greeting.

They walked towards each other, coming to a halt outside the café where they'd agreed to meet. Rosemary greeted her with a 'How're ye, Maureen?' But there was no hug or kiss on the cheek because Rosemary wasn't that sorta person.

'Grand, Rosemary. How's yerself?'

'I can't complain.'

Maureen knew from old that this was precisely what she was about to do. So, while her friend launched into an update on her creaking joints and clicking hip, Maureen adjusted the pram. The little girl had finally given in and nodded off as they reached the bottom of the hill. Her chubby cheek was lolling against her shoulder as Maureen eased the back of the seat down. Hopefully, now she'd catch up on some much-needed sleep while she and Rosemary chatted, she thought, contemplating the blanket. But, no, it was too warm for that; she'd leave her uncovered, an added bonus of which was her new dress was on display.

Maureen jumped in and interrupted Rosemary as she started in on the state of the Irish health system to point out her granddaughter's new pink frock. She relayed the battle she'd had with Moira over it and the compromise that had been reached. Rosemary got over her pique at being interrupted mid-rant when she rested her eyes on Kiera.

'Ah bless,' she said in a most un-Rosemary-like fashion.

It was further proof to Maureen that the babby Kiera was a shoo-in for the Rose of Tralee one day. The dress was duly admired, and the two women agreed that young mothers today didn't know they were born wanting to dress their babies in jeans and the like. Sure, Rosemary said hadn't she seen a babby boy with a bandana around his head like his mammy thought he was yer Bruce Springboard wan born in the USA? He was Irish, not American. They shook their heads at this sad state of affairs.

Pooh, fed up with not being given any attention, began to whine until Rosemary leaning on her pole with one hand, gave him a good scratch behind the ears. Then he emitted happy yips as she told him he was a good boy. Pooh had always had a soft spot for his mistress's friend. The feeling hadn't been mutual initially, but he'd won her over once his enthusiasm for snuffling where he had no business snuffling had been curbed.

'Hold the pram for me, would you, Rosemary, while I sort him out?' Maureen said, setting about securing her poodle to the lamp post. A bowl of water was placed outside the café for dog walkers who fancied a pit stop, and Pooh lapped it up. Then, still licking his chops, he sat down to begin his afternoon meet and greet session.

'Oh, she's precious. How old's your granddaughter?' A woman around about their own age was cooing over the pram.

'Eh-hem,' Maureen elbowed Rosemary out the way. 'My granddaughter's five months. And yes, she is precious.'

The woman smiled, and they passed a pleasant minute or two chatting about what a blessing grandchildren were. This time, Rosemary interrupted to tell them all about her granddaughter's prowess with waving the ribbons about in the rhythmic gymnastics. Maureen had heard it all before and tried not to look bored as she droned on.

Eventually, the woman, now an authority on the rhythmic gymnastics, announced she really must get on her way and, the lure of an afternoon coffee pick-me-up beckoned Maureen and Rosemary.

Rosemary held the door to the café open, and Maureen bustled inside with the pram. The interior was cool after standing in the sun, and the tantalising aroma of ground coffee beans along with a sugary, spice smell greeted them. A table towards the back of the nautically themed eatery was free, with room to park the pram so, Maureen made her way over to it, apologising to the man whose foot she ran over en route.

'I think I'll push the boat out and have an iced coffee with the fresh whipped cream,' Rosemary announced, checking out the menu board as Maureen appeared at her side.

Fresh cream was a weakness of Maureen's stemming from growing up in a village where there wasn't much but what they did have was fresh. Mind it was always her brothers who got first dibs on the cream off the top of the milk. It was their fault she'd no self-control around the stuff now.

Yes, she decided, she'd have what Rosemary was having. Sod the diet. It could start tomorrow. A pesky ten pounds was loitering around her middle, and she'd like to lose it before the party. It wouldn't do Donal any harm to shed a little weight either. The tyre around the belly wasn't good for a man to be carting about, either. Oh yes, starting tomorrow, it was the lean meat and salad leaves for them both, she vowed.

They were dipping into their frothy beverages when a mobile began to ring. Both women dived for their handbags, nearly knocking heads in the process, with Maureen holding her phone aloft triumphantly. 'It's mine, Rosemary, it's mine!' She hit the answer button and shouted victoriously into the little black device, 'Maureen O'Mara's mobile phone.'

'Jaysus wept, Mammy. Would you not bellow like so.'

'Sweet Mother of Divine, Aisling, is that you?'

Aisling sighed. Anyone would think she'd left on a ship for America years ago and was only now making contact. 'It's me, Mammy. I've rung to give you an update.'

'Where are you?'

'I'm out for lunch with Quinn.' Aisling wasn't going to divulge her exact whereabouts. If Mammy was in the locale, she might decide to join them.

'It sounds echoey like.'

'That's because I'm in the Ladies. It was too noisy in the restaurant.'

'You're not on the toilet, are you? Your sister was after ringing me while she was sat on the throne the other morning. I told her she was terrible rude.'

'No, Mammy, I'm not on the toilet. I'm beside the hand drier. Now, do you want to know what Doctor Kinsella said or not?' Aisling huffed. Her tomato soup would be a fecking chilled gazpacho at this rate.

'Of course, I do. I'm your mammy, aren't I? By rights, I should have been there with you this morning.'

Aisling ignored the wounded tone, getting straight to the crux of the matter. 'My tubes aren't blocked.'

'Thanks be to God! Rosemary, Aisling's falutin tubes aren't blocked.'

Rosemary, who had a cream moustache and hadn't the foggiest what Maureen was on about carried on dipping her spoon into the cream.

'So you can get back to the riding and let nature take its course now, Aisling?'

The cream went down the wrong way, and Rosemary erupted with a fit of coughing.

'Hold on there, Aisling, Rosemary's after choking.' Maureen put her phone down on the table and shot behind Rosemary to thump her on the back. The man with the hoop earring and scarf knotted about his head raced out from behind the counter toting a glass of water which he thrust at Rosemary. She snatched it from him and gulped it down before sitting back in her chair. Then, as she regained her equilibrium, she snapped, 'Would you stop thumping me, Maureen or I'll be adding the chiropractor to my list of appointments. I'm grand now, so I am.'

A chastened Maureen sat back down and picked up her phone once more. 'Are you still there, Aisling?'

'Yes, Mammy.' Aisling had decided her life wouldn't be worth living if she'd hung up on her.

'Rosemary was after choking on a spoonful of cream, but she's right as rain now. What else did Maggie have to say then?'

'She's going to run some blood tests to check on my ovary reserves as well as do some hormone tests. After that, I'll likely be started on a fertility drug.'

'She's after starting on the fertility drugs, Rosemary. Sure she'll be having triplets before we know it.'

Rosemary nodded, getting the gist of the conversation now.

'Mammy!'

'Well, it's good news, so.'

'It's not bad news exactly.'

'Then why don't you sound perkier?'

Aisling's shoulders slumped. Her body felt heavy with the weight of it all. 'It's nothing sorta news that's why, Mammy.' She bit her lip because she'd either scream or cry if her mammy told her she had to soldier on. Fortunately, no such platitude was forthcoming as Maureen waited for her to explain herself. 'If there was a problem with my fallopian tubes, then I'd know why I wasn't getting pregnant. I'm no wiser now than I was before I had the hyster,' it was too much of a mouthful, and she'd no energy to wrap her tongue around it, 'procedure.'

'Ah, Aisling, God's help is nearer than the door.'

That was a new one on her, Aisling thought, staring at the instructions on the hand drier. 'What's that supposed to mean?'

'I'll pray the rosary for you.'

'Thanks, Mammy.' Aisling injected a note of brightness she didn't feel into her words.

'That's better. Now then, before you go and have your lunch, I've some news that will cheer you up. I've decided on a theme for the housewarming party.' Maureen went on to tell her daughter about the Hawaiian luau. Her lips formed a thin line as she listened to Aisling's response before replying, 'No, you may not wear your swimsuit.'

After that, she said her goodbyes, casting an eye over Kiera, who was still sound asleep before picking up her spoon. She was about to dip into the frothy mess of cream atop her chilled drink once more when Rosemary raised an eyebrow that halted her in her tracks.

'Did I hear you right just now, Maureen? You've decided to host a Hawaiian themed party?'

'I have, Rosemary, and I'll tell you for why.' She explained the epiphany she'd had in the middle of the night.

Rosemary looked less than impressed when Maureen had another epiphany, having recalled there were volcanoes in Hawaii. 'You could come as one of those, erm excuse me,' she asked the pirate proprietor who was clearing the table nearby, 'what do they call those people who explore volcanoes?'

'Nutters.' He chortled at his own joke but sobered as Maureen didn't crack a smile. 'Erm, a volcanologist?'

'A volcanologist, that's it. Sure they need the hiking poles to get up and down the sides of the volcanoes so. You wouldn't have to worry about anyone else showing up in the same costume either.'

'I'm not wearing a spacesuit to your party, Maureen, and if you've ideas of me doing the hula, you can forget it.'

'It's a professional hula dancer we'll be after having, Rosemary,' Maureen sniffed before busying herself with her iced coffee. She made a mental note to make tracking down a hula dancer priority. Rosemary would never let her hear the end of it if she didn't follow through now.

Chapter Fourteen

'I think that weather will change before the day's done,' Maureen said, shivering as they veered down the side lane. You wouldn't even know it was there if you weren't in the know, she thought. The lane snaked off the main road, and it was single file only from hereon in. She envisaged herself and the pram becoming wedged in the narrow area shy of the shoe shop. But, still and all, at least she could always ring for help on her mobile.

Pooh was growling, low and throaty. It was his way of telling his mistress he'd have been perfectly happy to wait for them outside the café instead of down this back alley. What was he supposed to do here? He might have to cock his leg in protest.

The pram bumped over the cobbles, worn smooth by time, and a briny breeze straight off the sea whistled toward them. There was a nip to it which Maureen fancied foretold of bad weather at sea. She'd got skilled at the weather forecasting since she'd had a sea view but not good enough to have thought to bring a cardigan with her, she mused. She paused to pull the blanket up and around the still napping baby Kiera. 'There you go, my sleeping beauty. We can't have you cold now, can we? What would your mammy say?'

'These cobbles are murder on my hip, so they are,' Rosemary grumbled before coming to a halt outside the quaint shoe shop. She waited while Maureen, who gave quiet thanks for making it through the narrow gap, tethered Pooh to the lamp post. She promised the unhappy poodle they wouldn't be long, but he gave her a sceptical look, having heard that before.

Maureen straightened and took in the olde worlde shop they were about to enter. The door was painted a cheery blue, and Carrick's was printed in gold lettering above it. Beneath it in smaller type she read, Cobbling since 1925. Jaysus wept, yer little elf man must be a hundred if he was a day she thought, her gaze sliding to the window on the left-hand side. A black embossed leather handbag with gold tassels dangled from a hook. She rather liked the look of that she mused, being partial to tassels. Beneath the bag was a vase of colourful dried flowers along with three pairs of no-nonsense women's sandals in white, blue and black.

Maureen had only been inside the cobblers once before. The experience had put her in mind of those Wishing Chair books Aisling devoured as a child. There was yer man with the pointy little elf ears and a wizened expression who'd kept springing up from behind the counter like a jack-in-the-box. Then there was the wooden chair she'd perched in to try on a pair of bespoke boat shoes she'd have needed to re-mortgage the house to buy. She'd no intention of purchasing the shoes, wanting instead to see what warranted the hefty price tag. To be fair, they had been like walking on air, but she couldn't get them off her feet quick enough because it had been an unnerving experience sitting in the chair. She'd half expected it to suddenly sprout wings and fly off with her to the land of shoes or wherever. Not that she'd tell Rosemary any of that, she thought as her friend tried to dislodge her pole from between the cobbles. She'd say she was far too fanciful for her own good.

She brightened as it occurred to her that she might find suitable footwear for Donal inside the specialist footwear shop. Yes, they were sure to be pricey, but what price did you put on love? The flip-flops weren't safe for driving, and they made the most annoying noise when he flipped and flopped about the place. The sound was beginning to set her teeth on edge, and she didn't want to snap at the poor man; he'd enough on his plate or toe or whatever. Yes, she decided, she'd keep her eyes open for a smart but casual pair of sandals that would let the air get at that nail of his. He could wear them to the party.

'Maureen, don't stand there daydreaming,' Rosemary snipped as, having freed her pole, she pushed open the door to the cobbler's and, stepping inside the shop, set off a bell.

Maureen wrestled the pram in after her friend and was relieved to shut the door on the biting wind. She stood blinking as her eyes adjusted to the dim lighting. It was like stepping inside the Tardis from that Doctor Who show Patrick had been glued to as a lad, she thought, feeling a sneeze beginning to build. Dust tickled her nose, as did the pervasive scent of battered leather.

The sound of hammering drifted through a door behind the counter, and a cheerful voice from beyond called out, 'I'll be with you in a moment.'

The shelves were laden with shoes, and Maureen wondered if Mr Carrick had an army of little elves out the back helping him make them all. Before she could ponder this further, her eyes squeezed shut, and her nose wrinkled. 'Atishoo!'

'Bless you,' Rosemary tutted as she reached out to pluck a navy court shoe from the shelf, turning it over to inspect the heel. It was like a hot potato in her hand as she spied the price sticker, and she couldn't put it back on the shelf fast enough.

Maureen was about to move towards the wall displaying men's shoes to see what was to be found in the way of sandals. Before she could, the little man she remembered from her one and only previous visit materialised. He was definitely more elfin than leprechaunish, she decided as he beamed at them both. All he needed was a pointy hat with a bell on it and leggings under a tunic. No, she thought, catching sight of his midriff, perhaps not the leggings. That was not an image she wanted to spend time in her head. Instead, she focused her attention on the backdrop of stacked shoeboxes lining the wall behind the antiquated till. All were embossed with an art deco styled Carrick's logo. She felt as though she'd stepped back in time and wondered how Mr Carrick here survived in this day and age of chain store shops selling things on the cheap.

'Good afternoon, ladies. How can I be of service to you today?'

Maureen watched, bemused because it was like someone had flicked Mr Carrick's internal light switch as his dancing blue eyes alighted on Rosemary. His face lit up like a lighthouse beacon as he swept over her friend's practical all-weather walking attire and steel helmet hair. From the look on his face, she could have been wearing a ball gown.

'Ah, Mrs Farrelly! What a pleasure to see you again, and how would you be on this fine day?'

'Good afternoon, Mr Carrick. Well, for one thing, I'd be a lot happier if I had comfortable footwear, and I did tell you I'd be back in to reappraise the boots I asked you to hold for me.' Rosemary did not suffer fools gladly. 'I've brought my friend Maureen with me to give me a second opinion.'

Maureen nodded hello as Mr Carrick dragged his eyes from Rosemary to give her a cursory glance.

'I knew the moment I saw you that you'd be a wise woman, Mrs Farrelly. A second opinion doesn't hurt at all.'

'No, it doesn't.' Rosemary's tone was vinegary. 'Not given the prices you charge, Mr Carrick.'

Maureen would have liked to have snatched Rosemary's pole off her and jabbed her with it, but Mr Carrick was a man who could hold his own.

'Ah, now, Mrs Farrelly, 'tis no easy road in this day and age for a master craftsman who learned his trade at his daddy's knee. Sure there's a lot of love, time that goes into a pair of handmade Carrick's shoes, not to mention the finest quality materials.' He gestured about the shop. 'Stitched by my own two hands they are. Each and every pair.' He held up two work-worn, stubby hands. 'And they're made to last. A Carrick's shoe will last you a lifetime.'

Maureen didn't quite catch Rosemary's muttered reply as Mr Carrick said he'd fetch the boots for her. He disappeared out the back of the shop once more.

'You don't need to be so rude, Rosemary,' she said, telling her friend off.

'Stating the truth is not rude, Maureen.' There was a pious tilt to Rosemary's chin.

Again Maureen fought the urge to prod her with her pole. Miraculously, she managed to keep her sentiment that it was better to be a humble sinner than a self-righteous saint to herself, but only just.

'Here we are.' Mr Carrick sprang forth with a pair of no-nonsense boots in his hand.

To Maureen's eye, they were Rosemary to a T.

'A sturdier boot you won't find the length or breadth of the Emerald Isle.' He indicated the wishing chair. 'Please, have a seat, Mrs Farrelly.'

Maureen checked on Kiera, whose little mouth worked as she slept. She wondered what she was dreaming about as she risked a glance at Mr Carrick. Mercifully, he was wearing a pair of slacks and not green leggings.

Rosemary eased herself down onto the chair, her hip clicking as she did so, but Mr Carrick wasn't in the least fazed by his customer's bionic hip. On the contrary, he got down on bended knee with surprising ease for a man who had to be in his late sixties.

Maureen watched for a moment as he slipped off each of the sensible brown leather sandals adorning Rosemary's feet before deftly sliding a stocking sock over each. All the while, he cradled each of her white, relatively wide, clodhoppers with the beginnings of a bunion on the side of her left foot as though they were something precious. Now she knew how he competed with the big boys in the shoe world. Good old-fashioned service. It was hard to come by these days.

He really was going above and beyond the call of duty, she thought, taking a second look at the tableau. There was tension in the air. Now, she didn't claim to be an authority on body language and the like, but it was clear there was an animal attraction of sorts going on here. Mind, Rosemary was still looking sour. Still and all, the man could have a rose between his teeth, and she'd not pick up on it. She wasn't good at reading the signals wasn't Rosemary, which was why she'd missed out on Niall from their rambling group to that floozie, Bold Brenda. That and her being too miserable to stretch to the fancy trail mix

Brenda had tempted him with as they traversed the Howth hillside.

Yes, it was just as well she was here, she thought, forgetting all about sandals for Donal as she got down to the nitty-gritty of matchmaking. 'Tell me now, Mr Carrick,' she said slyly, 'Surely you're not after running this operation here all on your own? Is there a Mrs Elf, erm, Mrs Carrick working away behind the scenes?'

Mr Carrick struggled to tear his eyes away from Rosemary's stocking-clad foot, his good manners prevailing. 'Sadly now, Mrs Carrick passed some ten years back. So 'tis me all on my own, and I don't mind telling you it's a hard road being a widower. I spend my days engaged in the solitary business of shoes only to go home to a cold and empty cottage of an evening.'

'Ah, our sympathies, Mr Carrick. Rosemary and I are both widows. We know too well what it is to find yourself on your own facing a different future from what you'd planned. Although, I've a man friend these days myself.'

Rosemary shifted impatiently in the wishing chair.

Mr Carrick retrieved the boots, unlacing them before sliding them in turn to each expectant foot. 'They fit like a dream, so they do. Now, if you'd care to stand up, Mrs Farrelly, I'll lace them up for you, and you can have a trot around the shop.'

There was much clicking as Rosemary hauled herself up, leaning on her hiking pole. At the same time, Mr Carrick tightened the boot laces before tying a neat bow with practised ease at the top of each boot.

Maureen inspected the boots. Something odd was afoot, she thought, her eyes darting back and forth between the sturdy brown hiking shoes. She watched through narrowed eyes as Rosemary abandoned her pole to almost canter forth. What was going on? She frowned and turned to Mr Carrick with a question in her eyes. He tapped the side of his nose.

'It's a trade secret.'

'I want what she's got,' Maureen said. 'Sure, I've not seen Rosemary with such a spring in her step in a long while.'

'Ah well, now you look like a trustworthy sorta woman. Not the kind of woman inclined to gossip. Would I be right?'

'Yes, you'd be right there.' But, in her head, Maureen was already telephoning the rambling group. They needed to know about the miracle boots to be found at Carrick's the Cobblers.

'Tis all in the sole.'

Rosemary slowed her cantering long enough for Maureen to note a difference between the boots. One had a built-up heel. A special boot just for Rosemary.

Rosemary came to a halt, and Maureen wondered if she might toss her head and whinny.

'What do you think, Maureen?'

'I think those boots would be money well spent, Rosemary. The rate you're going there, you'll be doing the rhythmic gymnastics with your granddaughter in no time, so you will.'

'I can give you a ten per cent discount,' Mr Carrick cajoled.

'Fifteen per cent.'

'Done.' Mr Carrick looked at Rosemary admiringly. He liked a woman with a backbone, so he did.

Maureen knew if she didn't say something, Rosemary would leave the shop with her new boots, and that would be the last of her dealings with Mr Carrick. 'Tell me now, Mr Carrick, are you a man who enjoys a ramble?'

Rosemary's eyebrows shot up at the turn of phrase. Was Maureen propositioning the man? If so, she was being greedy, given she had Donal.

'I enjoy a good walk as much as the next man so long as I've a decent pair of Carrick's shoes on me feet, Mrs O'Mara.'

'Maureen, call me Maureen and Mrs Farrelly here, Rosemary.' God love him. Any man who'd been up close and personal with a woman's foot like so should be on a first-name basis with her. 'And that's grand, so it is because you know Rosemary and myself belong to a fine rambling group here in Howth. You'd be welcome to join us in discovering the delights of the Howth countryside.'

'Well, now then, if we're on a first-name basis, Maureen, you're to call me Cathal.' His twinkly gaze settled on Rosemary, who was side-eyeing Maureen. She strongly suspected she was trying to get a discount here at Carrick's for herself by luring yer man into the countryside. 'And I think I'd like that, Maureen.'

'Oh, and did I mention I'm after having a Hawaiian themed housewarming party in a couple of weeks? Sure, my man friend Donal and myself would be delighted if you'd attend.'

Chapter Fifteen

'I wasn't sure if you were joining us tonight, Ita,' Gaelic and Raw's choirmaster, Chris, announced as she burst into the church hall. The Silver Fox gave her a questioning look. He wore a plain gold wedding band, but no one had ever seen hide nor hair of his wife. Ita flashed him an apologetic smile.

If anyone else had greeted her like so, she'd have assumed they were being sarcastic. She knew this wasn't the case with Chris though. The retired music teacher was an even-tempered man. He always took the time to ask after each of their families and jobs, even if he was evasive about his own personal life. Her cardigan was quickly discarded, and she draped it over one of the chairs stacked three deep and lined up against the wall.

A soprano of indeterminable years, Angela was running through her scales, as was Pauline, a contralto, in the echoing hall. The slash of pink lipstick Angela favoured was, as per usual, as much on her front teeth as her lips, and Pauline's clip-on earrings were dragging her earlobes lower than her voice.

Breda, the pianist, a birdlike woman with fluttery hands, was flexing her fingers over the upright piano she was perched at, and chatter from the rest of the group hummed. It grew louder as voices competed to be heard over Angela's and Pauline's. Both women took their positions in the G N'R line-up with great seriousness. In one of his many pep talks, Chris had told the group that there were no stars in his choir, but the message hadn't sunk in where a certain two members were concerned. Both were convinced they were leading ladies. His leading ladies.

It had struck Ita as odd when she'd first joined the choir that these two straight-laced, widowed matrons should choose to be part of a choir such as G N'R. She'd had them pegged for a far more traditional church group. When she'd voiced this sentiment to Mags though, she'd laughed and told her the reason they warbled their way through Anastasia's hits and the like was because of Chris. They'd both got their sights set on him. Ita had felt a right eejit for missing the obvious.

The hall reeked of sausage rolls and coffee, and she guessed there must have been a function of some sort earlier. The sheet music she'd taken to pulling out at O'Mara's when the coast was clear to study was in her bag, and Ita retrieved it. She'd nearly learned all the songs they were to perform in Lisdoonvarna by heart now. Nearly being the operative word and as such, she wasn't ready to forego having the lyrics in front of her just yet.

The choir didn't usually practice on a Friday night. Friday evenings were set aside for socialising with friends or relaxing at home after the week. As the trip to the matchmaking festival loomed, though, the members of G N' R had agreed an additional practice wouldn't do them any harm. They all wanted to be pitch-perfect for their performance at the festival. So, when Chris telephoned around to say this was the only evening available at St Anne's, they'd all agreed.

Ita was happy enough to give up her Friday. She'd have only been out on the lash with Molly and Oonagh, and this way, she saved her pennies and woke up with a clear head. The thing with singing was she could have had the worst day, but when she joined in with the ebb and flow of voices as part of the choir, her mood would lift, and all her woes would float away. It was magical.

Now, she padded over to join the others in the black platform slides she'd bought new for summer and had worn to death. She slotted in between her fellow mezzo-soprano, Mags and Oisin, one of the five male tenors.

Mags gave her a gentle jab in the ribs as she whispered, 'You're cutting it fine, Ita. Those two are giving me a banging head. They've been at it for at least half an hour. They'll have no fecking voices left by the time we get underway.'

Ita grinned. 'Sorry.' She liked Mags. Not that she saw her or any of the others outside of choir practice apart from their Thursday evening pint at Madigan's down the road from the hall. She usually wound up sitting at the same table as Mags and Oisin. They were the closest in age and made an odd trio she often thought as she sipped on her ale. They all hailed from such different walks of life.

It was Mags who dominated the conversations, and she'd apologised for having so much to say for herself more than once. 'I know I've got the verbal diarrhoea, but honestly, if you'd been home all day with a four-year-old, you wouldn't shut up either.'

Ita had mouse-brown hair, and her catlike green eyes were her best feature, in her opinion, but they didn't make up for her pasty complexion. She was ordinary and didn't stand out in any way apart from when she sang. She'd have liked to have shopped at the fashionable high street stores or to have had Mags's flair for thrift shop fashion but more often than not, she frequented Penney's. Her mission, to hunt out a bargain to wear on her Friday nights. Once, she'd overheard her mam describing her as a bit of a wallflower and looking up what the phrase meant, she'd known it to be true. Oonagh and Molly turned heads and got chatted up while she was always overlooked. She wished she was flamboyant and loud like Mags, but she'd no clue how to be.

The girl on her left was in her late twenties with hair bleached a startling white and teased into a beehive. A diamanté stud decorated her nose, and she'd a penchant for colourful fifties frocks. She was a single mum to her son, Zeb and had made a point of telling Ita that when you were on your own like she was with Zeb, you had to be loud. If you weren't, she said, people would walk all over you.

Ita felt like people walked all over her. Sure, look at the way she was treated by those O'Mara girls. Oisin shuffled on her right. He was quiet and good looking in a nerdy sorta student way. He wore glasses and had hair a little too long that flopped into his eyes. She'd never seen him out of his battered old brown suede jacket. Ita could smell traces of cigarettes and beer on it now, not that he smoked. His jeans weren't the latest style but still fitted his lanky frame well, and she knew he enjoyed heavy rock music from his tee shirts. The one he'd worn to their previous rehearsal had been a nod to a Sound Garden concert. He'd told her and Mags he was in his third year at university studying history. One of these days, Ita would interrupt Mags and ask him what exactly he planned on doing with a degree in history.

'It's not like you to run late,' Oisin said.

Ita bristled. 'My aunt called from Canada as I was heading out the door, and I couldn't cut her short.' At any other time, she'd have been pleased to hear her aunt Ada's cheery voice down the line. She was fond of her mother's younger and only sister. Not that she'd seen her for years, but Aunt Ada always remembered her birthday and still sent her a little something each Christmas even though she was officially a grown-up now. She'd only been back to Ireland once since she and her husband Frankie, along with their two daughters, had left to forge a new life in Canada. Ita had been ten when they'd flown off on the aeroplane with her little cousins Tanya and Maddy. She'd tried not to cry at the airport and could remember her mammy and daddy waving madly as the family disappeared through the departure gates.

Kate Finnegan had turned to her husband when the doors slid shut behind them, 'Give it a year, and they'll be back.'

They hadn't been, though. Canada had suited them well.

Ita had always enjoyed hearing about the family's life over there. They all skied these days because that's what you did when you had the mountains on your doorstep. One day she'd like to visit. Maybe she'd be brave enough to try on a pair of skis too and try her luck. Perhaps if she went somewhere different, she could be different. Her meagre savings were a long way off affording a trip to Canada though.

She'd been grateful tonight when her mam had appeared and hovered until she'd passed the phone to her. It was a good thing she was heading out too because her mam always got terrible maudlin after chatting to Aunt Ada. She'd go on and on about what her life could have turned out like if she'd married someone solid and reliable like Ada's, Frankie. Someone who wouldn't trade his wife in for a younger model first chance he got. Ita thought it was high time her mam began to sing a different tune.

Hopefully, by the time she got in tonight, she'd be snoring in bed. That way, she'd be spared listening to her tired old monologue on what a waste of space Gerard Finnegan was.

'Will you come for a pint after? My mam's watching Zeb,' Mags asked.

'Why not.' The later she got home, the better Ita decided.

'What about you, Oisin?' Mags leaned over Ita. 'Will you come to Madigan's with us?'

'It'd be a sin not to.'

Chris cleared his throat, and as Angela and Pauline continued to warble, he cleared it louder. This time they went silent.

'Thanks be to God for small mercies,' Mags muttered, making Ita giggle.

'Good evening, everyone. Thanks a million for giving up your Friday night to be here. I've a few things to run through before we get started. The first is the festival organisers have confirmed our accommodation. We're being put up in twin-share rooms at Finney's Hotel.'

Gaelic and Raw weren't being paid to perform. Still, their bus fare to Lisdoonvarna and accommodation was being taken care of. Ita would have been stretched if she'd had to fork out, and she knew Mags would have had to bow out. Oisin as a student, couldn't be rolling in it either.

Mags nudged Ita again. 'You and I are sharing, right?'

Ita hesitated. She planned on sharing with her mam if she could convince her to come.

'Right?' Mags asked again.

'Right,' Ita said. She could sort out the rooming situation later.

'The hotel's a short bus ride from town,' Chris continued. 'I've a brochure to pass round.' He bent down and dug around in the brown case he always brought to practice. It reminded Ita of an old-fashioned doctor's bag, and she wouldn't have been surprised if, instead of a hotel brochure, he produced a stethoscope. Locating the glossy pamphlet, he passed it to Angela. Judging by her smug look down the line at Pauline, she took this as further evidence of being the leading lady at G N' R.

Heads turned to scrutinise Angela's face to see whether Finney's got the stamp of approval. She wasn't the sort who'd stay anywhere substandard.

'Perfectly acceptable,' she declared, and a collective sigh of relief went up as she passed the brochure to Penny next to her.

Chris's shoulders relaxed, and this time when he put his hand in his bag, he pulled out a tee shirt. 'This is the prototype we'll be wearing for our performance.'

The shirt was black with an emblem like that of the band Guns N' Roses, but the words Gaelic N' Raw were displayed above the rose and gun logo. The screen printer will have them ready mid-week.'

'They look great.' Tony, one of the tenors, stated his approval, and a murmur of consensus swept the group. They'd wear the shirts with black trousers and skirts. Ita and Mags had been unimpressed about wearing skirts, but Angela had been insistent to the point of stamping her foot. Pauline made noises about not blaming her for being averse to trousers. She'd said Angela could give yer rugby player man, Brian O'Driscoll, a run for his money on the field with her thighs. The rest of the female members, not wanting a skirmish to break out in the church hall, had quickly agreed to the skirts to pacify Angela.

'Pauline, are you still on board to pick them up?' Chris asked.

Pauline shot Angela a superior look before beaming at Chris with her lipsticked teeth. 'I am, Chris. You can rely on me. I won't let you down.'

'For feck's sake, yer woman will be licking his boots any minute now,' Oisin said under his breath.

Ita blinked. It was the sorta thing Mags would come out with, not the quietly spoken Oisin. Once she'd recovered from her surprise, a giggle escaped her lips.

'Grand, Pauline,' Chris said, shooting Ita a look that told her he knew exactly what had her amused.

Ita managed to straighten her face. Then, satisfied all was in order, Chris asked if anybody else had anything they wanted to say before they got down to the business end of their practice.

'Erm, I do.' Breda swivelled on her piano stool to face them all, her hands clasping and unclasping on her lap. 'I'm sorry to have to let you down at such short notice, but I'm not able to come to Lisdoonvarna.'

A collection of 'oh nos' and 'why nots?' went up.

Breda pinkened and looked slightly ill. She explained her husband had been given a date for his hernia operation, and it was scheduled for the day they were due to leave.

'Of course. You can't possibly come, Breda.' Chris overrode Angela, who was making noises about Breda telephoning the hospital to see if the surgery could be rescheduled. 'We understand, don't we.'

Angela, chastened, nodded, as did the others. However, they were all in silent agreement that Breda pulling out was a disaster. Where would they find a pianist who could play their repertoire with the ease Breda did at such short notice?

A fizzing sensation shot through Ita, and she bit down on her lip to temper it. She couldn't believe her luck, but now wasn't the time to broach her idea. Instead, she'd bring it up after practice.

'You're not to be worrying now, Breda. We'll sort something out,' Chris told the contrite pianist before announcing that they'd run through the songs in order of their planned performance. Breda's bombshell was put aside as folders were opened and sheets rustled in readiness. Chris took a deep breath, 'Right, from the beginning.' He nodded to Breda. She, in turn, glad to get on with things, began to play the intro they were all familiar with.

Ita felt Mags next to her sway to the music, and she licked her lips in readiness for their cue. It came when Chris waved his hand up, and the Gaelic and Raw choir duly began harmonising along to their version of 'Sweet Child O' Mine'.

Chapter Sixteen

I t was after nine by the time Chris switched off the lights
inside the hall. First, he pulled the main door shut
before locking it. Then, checking the handle once more as
was his custom, he turned to face an evening suffused in
the soft-focus of twilight.

The small group who'd opted to quench their thirst at
Madigan's were already halfway to the pub. A sigh escaped
his lips as he spied Pauline and Angela lurking under the
tree in the churchyard. They were like birds of prey circling,
so they were, and he twisted the plain gold band on his
finger in irritation. Ita usually set off for the pub with Mags
and Oisin, so he was surprised to see she'd hung back too.
Surprised and pleased because there was safety in
numbers.

Ita wished the two women, who between them
probably kept the staff of Boots Ireland in full-time
employment with the amount they'd spent on hairspray
over the years, would disappear. Honestly, she thought a
tornado wouldn't lift a hair on either of their coiffed heads.
She wanted to talk to Chris about her idea, and she didn't
want those two earwigging.

'Your voice was in fine fettle this evening, Ita,' Chris
stated as, pocketing the keys, he took the three steps
down to join the trio where they waited near the gate.

Angela and Pauline looked put out and Ita felt the
warmth spread across her cheeks. She knew she'd turned
a mottled pink at the compliment. Her mam had told her
on more than one occasion she needed to learn how to be

gracious. It was true enough. All she had to do was say a simple thank you, but somehow it always came out sounding wrong when she did so—like she thought the praise was her due or something. So to cover her awkwardness, she decided not to beat around the bush.

'Erm, Chris, I wondered if I could have a word.' She glanced at Angela and Pauline, hoping they'd get the hint. But instead, they both took a step closer.

'Certainly. Angela, Pauline,' he said jovially, 'why don't you set off, and we'll catch you up. Sure, we won't be far behind.'

Ita flashed Chris a grateful smile.

However, neither woman moved. Instead, both had seemingly taken root like the leafy maple they were standing under. Chris frowned and cleared his throat; this time his voice brooked no argument. 'We'll catch you up then.'

His tone penetrated and reluctantly the two older women allowed him to usher them out the church gate. Their pace was slower than a snail's as they set off down the street with Pauline enquiring how Angela was faring with her neighbour. Apparently, he'd been complaining about her practising her scales in the bathroom. It was unfortunate the bathroom window overlooked his back garden.

'Do I complain about his lying on that sun lounger of his in his scanty pants? No, I do not.' Angela stated indignantly.

Chris was trying not to laugh as he turned his attention to Ita and looked at her expectantly.

She was suddenly anxious because she needed to make this happen. 'What it is, erm well, what I wondered was, perhaps I could ask my mam to stand in for Breda in Lisdoonvarna?'

'Your mam plays the piano?'

'She does, yes.' He didn't need to know Kate Finnegan hadn't played a note since her husband had left, determined, in Ita's opinion, to stay miserable forever.

'And do you think she'd manage the songs we're planning on performing alright?'

'I do.' Ita's nod was emphatic. Surely playing the piano was like riding a bike? Once you knew how you never forgot.

Chris thought this might be the answer to his prayers, and the load lightened on his shoulders at the prospect of not having to hunt down a pianist at such short notice. 'Well then, yes, by all means, ask away.'

Excitement at the way things were panning out surged. 'I will then,' Ita smiled widely.

She'd be a pretty girl if she smiled more often, Chris thought as they followed after Angela and Pauline.

'Ah, there you are,' Angela said, waiting for the choirmaster to fall into step alongside herself and Pauline.

Ita was happy to trail a little behind because her mind was whirring. She couldn't hang about waiting for the right moment to broach the topic with her mam because Chris would need a definitive yes or no answer as soon as possible. Still and all, she'd have to be wise as to how she went about it. There was no point blurting it out before her mam had her morning cup of tea!

Hmm, now that was an idea. Perhaps that's what she should do. The last time she'd taken her mam a cup of tea in bed had been Mother's Day. Sure, she'd been delighted. Well, as delighted as her mam ever was over anything. Yes, she resolved. She'd take her a cup of tea in bed tomorrow morning. There was a skip to Ita's step. She really couldn't believe what good luck Breda's cancelling was because now she'd the perfect excuse to take her mam with her to Lisdoonvarna. Best of all, Kate Finnegan wouldn't suspect a thing.

A burst of laughter brought Ita back to the here and now as the door to the pub swung open. A group of lads stumbled forth and Chris caught the door before it closed and held it open. Angela and Pauline each gave him a flirtatious smile then they were enveloped in the smoky atmosphere of the pub. Ita thanked him and stood inside the doorway, taking stock for a moment.

Given it was Friday night, it was busier than usual. People shouted in each other's ears, trying to be heard over the top of one another, but there was no music playing as yet. That would come later, Ita guessed, seeing the corner area where chairs were arranged in a semi-circle for the musicians. A lonely fiddle was resting against one of the seats, the bow on the chair waiting to be played. She swept the crowded interior and caught Mag's eye as she made her way to the bar. She waved and Mags pointed in the direction where she'd just been looking. Then, on a second appraisal, she caught sight of Oisin, who'd somehow managed to nab them a table next to where the music would be played later.

'Oisin's over there,' Ita said in case Chris wanted to join them. He was already being dragged away by Pauline and Angela. Madigan's wasn't the sort of establishment either woman would frequent by choice. They'd be more at home in a wine bar or cocktail lounge, but a sticky floor and the smell of ale were a small price to pay for a few extra hours in their choirmaster's company.

Ita pressed past a group of giggling girls to where Oisin was guarding a table. He pushed his glasses back up his nose and grinned up at her as she pulled a chair out. Above his head, a cluster of framed photographs depicting the various musicians who'd played in the pub through the years adorned the wall. She sank down into the seat. 'God, it's mad in here tonight.'

'It'll only get madder when the music starts later on,' Oisin replied, smoothing the beer mat he'd been toying with flat on the table. He looked at Ita properly then. 'You're looking pleased with yourself. What was it you were after talking to Chris about?'

She couldn't help the smile spreading across her face. 'That's because I am. I think I've solved the problem of Breda.'

'Really?'

'Really.'

'How? You don't play, do you?' His expression was curious.

'No, not me. My mam does though.' Ita hesitated. Should she tell him about her matchmaking plan? She didn't know him that well after all.

Mags appeared at that moment, carrying three pint glasses. She set them down on the table.

'And not a drop spilt. I'll have you know.' Mags did a Sunday lunchtime shift at a pub to top up her meagre income. She'd mentioned they were looking for extra bar staff to Ita a few weeks back, given she'd complained about her wages at O'Mara's and the cost of living in Dublin. Ita had no wish for a second job, though. She also knew she'd have slopped half the contents of the glasses had she attempted to carry three at one time. She'd be a useless barmaid. Besides, she couldn't move out of home until she'd her mam sorted.

'I'm gasping,' she said, wetting her lips on the drink.

Mags glanced about and muttered. 'Ah, Jaysus, those two don't give the poor man a minute's peace. Look at them over there fawning all over him, would you.'

Ita didn't need to track Mags' gaze to know she was talking about Chris, Angela and Pauline.

'I hope his room has a good lock on it down in Lisdoonvarna,' Oisin muttered, making both Mags and Ita splutter into their pints.

They whiled away a few minutes laughing at the thought of the pair of them in their nightgowns sneaking about the hotel after midnight trying to locate Chris's room.

'His wife might be going with him for all we know,' Mags said. 'I wonder what she's like?' she added as an afterthought. 'Have either of you ever seen her?

Both Ita and Oisin shook their heads.

'I'd imagine her to be elegant and quietly spoken,' Ita said.

'And not have lipstick on her teeth,' Mags added.

'Or earlobes down to her knees.' Oisin wasn't to be left out.

They laughed once more.

'Well, they say there's someone for everyone, and sure aren't we off to a matchmaking festival.' Mags shrugged. 'It's a shame about Breda not being able to come. I hope the whole thing doesn't get panned. I'm so looking forward to a break. It's the first time I'll have been on my own for longer than a night since Zeb was born. Not that I'll be on my own. We'll be sharing a room, Ita, and I promise I don't snore. Well, not too loudly anyway!' She dug her phone out, planting it on the table.

Ita opened her mouth, intending to say that if things went to plan, she wouldn't be sharing with Mags but rather her mam, but the other girl was away again.

'I won't be able to hear it if it rings otherwise. My mam couldn't sit tonight, so I've my neighbour's daughter looking after Zeb, and I left her strict instructions to phone me if she'd any problems.'

Oisin took a sip of his pint and then said, 'Ita's after suggesting her mam stand in for Breda in Lisdoonvarna.'

Mags raised a dark eyebrow. It was at odds with her white hair. 'Your mam plays the piano?'

'She does, erm, well she did.' Ita studied the contents of her glass.

'What do you mean?' Oisin asked.

She looked from him to Mags and decided she had to share what she had up her sleeve with someone.

'My mam used to play the piano all the time. Just for pleasure like but she was really good. She stopped when I was fourteen, and my dad left.'

'She stopped playing the piano because of a broken heart?' Mags asked.

Ita nodded. 'I suppose she did.'

'So what makes you think she'll want to take it up again after all these years?'

'And publicly,' Oisin added.

'I'm going to tell her there's nobody else and if she doesn't step in, we'll have to pull out of the festival.'

Oisin's brown eyes studied her from behind his lenses. 'I get the feeling it's not only about helping the choir out?'

Ita chewed her lip for a moment and then made her mind up. She'd told them this much she might as well tell them the rest. Besides, it was different talking to Oisin and Mags. It wasn't like she knew them of old. They were impartial. 'I know it sounds silly, but you know all about Lisdoonvarna's matchmaker, right?'

'Sort of,' Mags replied.

'I've heard of him,' Oisin said.

Ita repeated what she'd read about the country's most famous matchmaker, whose presence at the annual festival was a huge drawcard. You could find him in his office, a corner of the Matchmaker Bar, throughout September. He was a third-generation matchmaker, and according to what Ita had read, he'd successfully paired over three thousand couples. Surely that meant there was hope for her and her mam.

'I want my mam to touch his magic book. It's over one hundred and fifty years old, and it's believed that if you touch it with both hands, keep your eyes closed for eight seconds and think about love, then it will come your way.' She flushed, hearing herself say it out loud.

Mags snorted. 'You don't believe all that, do you?'

Ita shrugged. 'I don't know.'

'Sure, the world would be a boring place if we knew everything,' Oisin said, and Ita flashed him a grateful smile.

'One thing I do know,' she said, 'is my mam's been miserable for years now, and I want her to be happy again.' But, she didn't add, I want to be happy again, too. She'd spent so long punishing her dad for leaving, having convinced herself if she was awful enough, Francine would get fed up and leave him. Her simplistic teenage mind had thought her dad would come home to her mam then, and things could go back to how they used to be. But, of course, that hadn't happened.

'Are you alright, Ita?' Oisin asked gently.

She could see the concern in his eyes, Mags too when she looked uncertainly to her.

'Sometimes it helps to talk about things,' Oisin said.

Ita took a deep breath and found herself opening up about what had happened after her father left.

Chapter Seventeen

Dublin, 1993

At first, Ita had gone to stay at her dad's smart new flat in trendy Portobello every Friday night, catching the bus there after school. The Dublin 8 address didn't suit him, she decided, the first time she hopped off the bus to walk to his two-bedroom apartment. It was full of yoga studios, bookshops, upscale bars, and eateries where people sat to be seen and ate things like brunch on a Saturday morning. It did not suit the dad she knew. So much so that she wondered if she'd ever known him at all.

He'd been so keen for her to like the apartment on the top floor of a three-storey block, but she'd refused to be impressed. Her expression had remained disdainful as he demonstrated the modern fittings, and she'd shown no wonderment over the fact you could see the Grand Canal on a good day without moving from the living room sofa. And, if he'd expected her to be impressed by the curtains, cushions and bedding in her room the woman from the homewares store had assured him were perfect for a teenage girl, then he'd have been sorely disappointed.

It was hard seeing him in different surroundings. Ita couldn't get used to the edgier clothes he'd taken to wearing either. In her opinion, they made him look like a desperate middle-aged man instead of her dad. He'd be driving about in some sort of shiny black convertible next with music blaring as he slowed to a stop at the lights. The hardest thing of all, though, was Francine or Frankie for short. She was the woman he'd left her mam for. Ita would never, ever get used to her living under the same roof as her father.

Francine, Ita refused to call her by her nickname like everyone else, was fifteen years younger than Gerard Finnegan. Nicknames were, to Ita's mind, what you gave people you considered friends or family. Francine was neither. She was the woman who'd stolen her mam's husband and her father. She was the woman who'd ruined their lives.

Her mam said Francine was cheap and brassy, and when Ita asked her how she knew what she looked like, Kate had remained tight-lipped on the subject. This had put the fear in Ita. Had her mam taken it upon herself to visit the offices above the factory and give them a piece of her mind? The scene in Ita's head was like something from an American soap opera. It was all too horrible to contemplate, and she'd not delved deeper.

Francine was attractive. She'd concede that. Her blonde hair was straightened, and her lips and nails were painted a glossy rose colour. Francine looked after herself and wore clothes and shoes that Ita herself coveted. In fact, she'd have loved to have practised walking about in a pair of her father's girlfriend's stilettos. Francine wore heels all the time, even at home.

To be fair, Francine tried hard with her, fussing over her when she came to stay and making sure the cupboard was stocked with her favourite junk foods. But Ita wouldn't be bribed.

'Ita, there's a packet of Tayto cheese and onion in the cupboard. Your dad said you like them. Don't be shy. Help yourself.'

'I don't like that flavour anymore, and besides, my mam says crisps will give me spots,' Ita sneered. It wasn't true on both counts, and it had been torturous, but she'd not touched the bag of crisps. To do so would be to let her mam down.

'Ita, why don't you invite your friends over? Gerard and I want you to feel this is as much your home as it's ours,' Francine had chirped one Friday night as they forked up their plates of Chinese takeaway. Her dad had nodded enthusiastically, eyes alight at the idea. 'That's a grand idea, Frankie. Ita, why don't you ask Molly and Oonagh if they'd like to call around and see your old man's new gaff. Frankie would love to meet the girls too.'

Francine was in danger of dislocating her neck, so heartily did she nod her agreement.

Ita didn't look up, mumbling through her mouthful of fried rice, 'Yeah, maybe.' She'd never think of the apartment as her home. How could she? Nevertheless, she'd asked Oonagh and Molly around for the afternoon a few Saturdays later because she was desperate for company. Her dad had been embarrassing in his enthusiasm at seeing her school friends. Likewise, it had been cringeworthy when he demonstrated the surround sound of his new stereo by putting Moby on. The girls, however, had been dutifully impressed. The thing Ita hadn't expected though, was for them to be so smitten with Francine.

'Frankie's really pretty,' Molly gushed, her hand in the bowl of crisps as she sat on the floor of Ita's bedroom. There were snacks aplenty in the kitchen bought by Francine, and if Ita refused to be bought, Molly and Oonagh certainly didn't have a problem. Molly wiggled her toenails, admiring their rosy glow as she waited for the varnish to dry. When she'd mentioned how much she liked the colour of Francine's fingernails to her, Francine insisted Molly borrow the Sally Hansen varnish.

'It's Francine, not Frankie,' Ita sniped.

'But she asked us to call her Frankie,' Molly replied bewildered.

'And, you know what's really cool?' Oonagh added, her tongue poking out of the corner of her mouth as, having commandeered the polish from Molly, she counted three strokes on each toe. 'I bet she'll let you borrow her clothes when you want, too. I love the bell sleeves on that top she's wearing.'

'Yeh, you're actually lucky how things have worked out if you look at it like that, Ita,' Molly said, shovelling the handful of crisps in. 'You'll get loads of Christmas presents too because kids whose parents have split up always do.'

Ita had shouted she didn't care about things like that as she bit the head off both her friends. They slammed off home, and she'd not spoken to either of them for a week. It was the longest week of her life. She'd never felt so alone, and in the end, she'd said she was sorry. This was despite meaning every word she'd said because she didn't want to lose her two best friends as well as her dad.

They'd made it up and Ita had pinched Francine's nail varnish as payback because it was her fault she'd had to grovel to Molly and Oonagh. She'd denied knowing anything about the polish when Francine asked her if she'd seen it.

Francine had looked at Ita in a way that told her she knew she was lying, but Ita knew she wouldn't push her on it. She'd keep the peace for her dad's sake. It had given her a sense of power where before she'd felt powerless.

The months rolled by and Ita didn't soften towards her father's girlfriend. How could she when her poor mam was heartbroken, still sobbing herself to sleep at night? So, she'd not felt the slightest remorse as she sprayed Francine's expensive bottle of Gucci perfume out the bathroom window until there was only a smidge left at the bottom. She'd waltzed off home with a top she fancied too, and so it had gone on.

Her dad had tried to talk to her about her behaviour. 'I know it's been hard for you to accept your mother and I separating, Ita, but this animosity towards Frankie, it's got to stop.'

Ita told him it wasn't her. It was Francine trying to turn him against her. She'd sobbed out that she was trying to poison her daddy against her. She could see he was torn, but she'd not felt badly over her behaviour because he'd no clue what it was like for her. He'd caused all this. It was down to him she dreaded going home on a Saturday and seeing her mam's wounded eyes. Accepting the situation and allowing Francine into her life would hurt her mam further, and she'd been hurt enough.

Finally, things came to a head on a Saturday afternoon when Ita had been particularly scathing over Francine's choice of DVD for a planned movie night in. Something had snapped in Francine and as Ita took herself off to her bedroom, she heard her shout at her father.

'I can't take it anymore, Gerard. This isn't how I thought things would be. Do something or I'm leaving!' She'd burst into noisy sobs.

Ita, lurking in the doorway of her bedroom, held her breath as she tried to catch what her father was saying, but his voice was too soft. Finally, she gave up and shut her bedroom door, flopping down on the bed and staring up at the ceiling. She'd thought she'd feel jubilant at having finally pushed Francine to breaking point, but she felt dead inside.

The thing she'd never admit to anyone, least of all her mam, was that she might have liked Francine in another life. You see, she'd a laugh that made you want to laugh along with her, and people gravitated towards her like she was a patch of sunlight on a cold day. Francine also genuinely seemed to love her dad and not for his money, as her mam said. This was a stretch anyway because while he was comfortable enough, he was hardly rolling in it.

Her mam was still of the mindset that her husband had had a mid-life crisis. 'It happens,' she'd say through pursed lips. 'He'll be back with his tail between his legs. You'll see, Ita. Things will be back to normal before you know it.'

This was what Ita had hoped for, longed for, but now that she'd pushed Francine to the point of leaving, she wasn't so sure it was what she wanted anymore. A frisson of anger at her mother had stirred as she'd stared at the Chinese paper lantern light shade dangling from her ceiling. Why couldn't she move on? Ita had tried to recall hearing her dad singing in the shower or whistling as he strode about their house like he did now. He looked younger too because being happy was the best tonic to age there was. Would coming home mean he'd be miserable? Was that what she'd wanted?

Things didn't work out like Ita thought they would because Francine didn't leave her dad. He didn't come home to her mam either.

What happened instead was this.

Her father tapped on Ita's door an hour or so after Francine's explosion. It was good timing because she was beginning to feel hungry but hadn't been game to venture out of her bedroom to see how the land lay.

'Come in,' she called out, pulling herself upright and resting her back on the headboard. She stared anxiously as the door opened, wondering if it was her dad on his own or whether Francine had come to talk to her as well.

It was just her father with a slump in his shoulders that suggested he felt beaten down. He shut the door behind him and sat down on the end of the bed. His face looked grey and drawn, Ita thought, and for the first time, a pang of guilt at the way she'd been acting shot through her. She plucked at the duvet, waiting to hear what he'd say.

'Ita, love, it's not working out too well, is it?'

'What do you mean?' She tensed, unsure what direction he was going in.

'This,' he gestured around the room. 'You staying over. It's not working.'

'I don't understand.' And she didn't. This was not how things were supposed to go.

'Ah, come on now, Ita, you're not a silly girl. I can see you're unhappy when you're here.'

Ita opened her mouth to protest, but her dad silenced her with his hand. 'Let me finish.'

She clamped her mouth shut, clenching her jaw tight.

'That's why I think it would be better if you didn't stay anymore.'

Ita's stomach plummeted, the way it did when the car dropped down the other side of a hill too fast, 'But, Dad—'

'Listen, love. It doesn't mean I love you any less, or I don't want to see you. That's not the case, but this is Frankie's home too, and I have to think of her as well.'

'But you said this was my home as well.'

He looked stricken. 'Ah, Ita, it still is, but things can't carry on the way they have been.'

Ita scrabbled to find the words to fix things. This wasn't what she wanted, but the words wouldn't come. She watched as he clapped his hands and then rubbed them together as though satisfied that was all sorted.

'What I thought would be grand would be you and I having a date each Saturday. We could go to Eddie Rockets. You love their burgers. What do you think of that?'

He looked as though he expected this to be greeted with the same enthusiasm it would if he'd suggested a trip to Disneyland.

Ita nodded slowly, her throat aching and tight. There was no one to blame for this but herself.

'Ita, there's something else.'

Ita blinked. She didn't want him to see her cry. 'What?'

'Frankie's pregnant. You're going to have a little sister or brother.'

Chapter Eighteen

Present Day

'I don't see him anymore.' Ita finished talking with a shrug.

Initially, her dad had picked her up regular as clockwork on Saturdays at midday. She'd see the net curtain twitching as her mam watched them drive away, and feel torn like she was somehow letting her down.

The weekly pilgrimage to Eddie Rockets on O'Connell Street was strained and the burgers and fries which had always set Ita's mouth watering tasted like cardboard. She felt doubly betrayed because not only had he wrecked her mam's life, he'd made it clear that Francine and the new baby were his priority now.

Ita took a long pull on her pint, becoming aware of her surroundings once more as the clinking of glasses and chatter around them seemed to grow louder.

There'd been something cathartic about owning up to how awful she'd been to Francine. As an adult, she could see her behaviour had been intolerable. It was all so screwed up, and she'd never told anybody the whole truth of it. What would Oisin and Mags think of her now, though? she wondered, almost afraid to look up.

'It wasn't your fault,' Oisin said. 'You were a kid who was caught in the middle of her parents' break-up.' He trod carefully, not wanting to voice that from the outside looking in, if anyone was to blame, it was Ita's mam. She'd been so caught up in her own misery, she'd dragged her daughter down in it with her. She'd behaved selfishly.

'Divorce is ugly,' Mags added as though she'd first-hand experience of it herself. 'What about the baby though?' Her expression was curious as to how the rest of Ita's story had played out. 'How did your mam take her arrival?'

'Her name's Eve. She's eight now. I don't see her either. I don't see any of them except my mam, of course, and she didn't take it well because she had to accept it then. Dad wasn't coming back to her, us.'

Ita remembered when her half-sister was born. Her dad had brought her up to see Eve in the hospital. Despite herself, she'd been so excited to meet her new sister. Eve was tiny, like a raisin with a loud squalling cry. She'd sat down in the chair beside Francine's bed as the baby girl was placed carefully in her arms, and her heart had melted with the privilege of being entrusted to hold her.

It was a sliding doors moment because Ita sensed as she cooed over Eve that she was at a crossroads with Francine. She could have let Eve's arrival build a bridge between them. It was a bridge that would ultimately lead her back to her dad, but her mam's voice had echoed in her ears. You watch, he'll forget all about you now he's a new family.

The moment came and went.

The look on her mam's face when her dad had telephoned to cancel their Eddie Rockets Saturday for the first time said, I told you so.

'He's got to help Francine with the new baby, Mam,' Ita had protested, but Kate simply tightened her lips.

One missed Saturday stretched into two then three until she was lucky to see him once a month.

She'd have liked a relationship with her younger sister. It wasn't easy being at home with only her mam, but there was too much water under the bridge now.

That little voice belonging to her conscience had told her it was her own doing. She'd turned Francine against her with her behaviour. But her dad could have fought harder to stay in her life. It hurt that he hadn't cared enough. Life could be unfair, and it seemed to Ita it had dealt her a rough hand. She wanted to be the little girl who'd trusted in others and believed that come what may things would be alright because she was loved. That was what she'd lost when her dad had left her mam for Francine. Trust.

'I saw Eve a few times when she was little. She was a dote, but then things got worse with mam.' She pictured the afternoon she'd called around to see her dad and Eve. They'd been in the living room. She was sitting stiffly on the sofa, and her dad was holding Eve by both hands, helping her toddle across the living room. The rain was tapping against the doors to the small veranda, and there'd been no chance of seeing the Grand Canal on such a drizzly, gloomy day.

Francine was at the hairdressers having a well-earned break, her dad said when he rang to ask if she'd like to pop round for the morning. On the rare occasions she did see him, Francine was always out. He'd lost weight, she thought, eyeing him as he encouraged Eve. The paunch around his middle had disappeared. She supposed he was doing his best to stay trim and fit for his young family.

Her baby sister's sturdy, determined legs as she planted one foot uncertainly down after the other made her smile, but then she lifted her gaze back to her father. A pain so sharp stabbed her at the look of adoration on his face as he concentrated on Eve. Had he ever looked at her like that?

He was oblivious to Ita's thoughts as he blithely announced, 'An apartment's no place to bring up children. Eve and her baby brother or sister are going to want a garden to run about in.'

Ita recoiled as though she'd been slapped.

'Francine's expecting again.' He beamed.

She hadn't congratulated him, her face stony.

Sitting here in Madigan's, she could still see the cloud that had passed over his face.

'My mam was apocalyptic when he told her she'd have to sell the house and downscale.' Ita shuddered at the memory. 'It rubbed salt in the wound when they moved along with the new baby, Heidi, to a house in Ranelagh with a garden while all Mam could afford was a terrace. Not that there's anything wrong with the house, in my opinion. There's only the two of us. Sure, why would we need anything bigger? It's just that—'

'Your mam refuses to be happy.'

'That's it exactly,' Ita said to Oisin. He got it.

'I didn't see him at all after Heidi was born. I was nearly seventeen by then and,'—she shrugged—'I suppose I felt like an inconvenience.' But, to her mind, her mam's words about Gerard Finnegan forgetting her now he had a new family were prophetic.

'Would you like to see them?' Oisin asked.

Ita stared into the dregs of her glass. That was the thing. She would, but she'd no clue how to go about it. How could she find her way back to her father now after all that had happened?

Chapter Nineteen

'Bearach and I are going to try and make the salsa night next week,' Leila chirped down the phone. 'It's been ages since we all caught up.'

'You should. It's fun,' Aisling replied, trying to sound enthusiastic. She and Quinn had been to two of the Tuesday evening dance nights where the flamboyant Lonzano's opened their Dame Street studio for a salsa free-for-all.

She was stretched out on the sofa with the television on quietly in the background. A weekend omnibus of the soaps was the only thing worth having on. A half-drunk cup of tea and an open packet of Snowballs were on the coffee table. She'd the phone pressed to her ear, half-listening as Leila chattered on. Her hand occasionally snaked out for a Snowball.

Moira, Tom and Kiera had gone to his parents for Sunday lunch, and Quinn was at the restaurant where he'd eat on the go. In days of old, Aisling would have relished having the apartment to herself for a rare lazy Sunday afternoon. She might have painted her toenails and binged the soaps before heading out to meet friends for a Sunday session in Temple Bar. Today, though, the apartment felt empty.

She could have wandered down to Quinn's where the staff were well used to seeing her perched on a stool in the kitchen. There she could munch on a plate of whatever took her fancy while watching her husband work, but she hadn't been in the mood for all that busyness. And the thought of having to think of a witty comeback with the bistro's quite mad but highly entertaining maître de, Alisdair, was exhausting.

Going out would mean changing into something other than the Mo-pants she was currently sprawling in. Somehow she'd managed to get melted chocolate on them. She'd changed into her sloth attire after having helped James, the student who worked the weekend reception day shift, over the busy checking-out time downstairs.

O'Mara's was in for a quiet afternoon with no check-ins until a tour group arrived the following morning. If there were any walk-in guests, then James was perfectly able to check them in himself. There was no point in her loitering downstairs annoying him.

There'd not seemed much point going to any bother for lunch either, not when she was the only one home. She was trying to eat all the foods the pamphlet she'd picked up from the doctors stated were good for fertility, but couldn't be arsed today. Snowballs it was. If she were honest, the chocolate marshmallow treats were a welcome break from all the salmon, lentils, seeds and avocados she'd been quaffing. She'd always loved salmon, but that was when she ate it once a week, not three to four times, and despite chomping the pink fish down and eating all those other healthy foods, according to the test she'd sneakily done that morning, she still wasn't going to be spawning any time soon.

Aisling had known it was silly to do the test. She was setting herself up to fail because she'd only finished her period a week ago, but it had been a compulsion because, well, because you never knew. Women could still bleed while they were pregnant. So, she'd waited until Moira and Tom were busy with Kiera, and Quinn had left to pop in on his parents before heading to the restaurant. Then she'd unearthed the kit hidden beneath the pile of winter jerseys in her drawer and had taken herself off to the loo.

A grey cloud had hovered over her day after having seen that single blue line, and she'd not been able to shake it off. Her usual sunny good humour and the efficiency she prided herself on when it came to running O'Mara's had deserted her that morning downstairs. She couldn't be bothered. It all felt too hard. Luckily, she'd not had to deal with any awkward guests quibbling over their bill either because she really didn't trust herself to maintain a pleasant facade.

James had picked up on her mood, which was surprisingly observant for a teenaged lad, and tears had threatened when he asked her if everything was alright. She'd blinked them back furiously, knowing she wouldn't confide in him even if she had been able to pinpoint what the matter was. There wasn't one particular thing wrong, that was the problem. It was more a lethargy creeping over her of not giving a toss. Perhaps she should have spoken to Ita about how she was feeling. She was the queen of inertia.

'Ash?'

Aisling blinked. She'd zoned out of her conversation with Leila. What was she on about? One of her brides-to-be who was currently driving her demented, that was it. Her best friend ran a successful wedding planner business, and this time of year, things were hectic for her. They'd only caught up for snatched conversations these last few months with Aisling keeping Leila in the fertility loop and Leila regaling her with love-struck updates as to her boyfriend, Bearach.

This afternoon with everybody out and nothing on tele to hold her attention had seemed the perfect time to give her friend a call. They were long overdue for a good chat.

'Sorry, Leila, I am here.'

Leila sighed. She knew precisely what Aisling was thinking about it. 'Ash, I'm sure if you stopped thinking about getting pregnant all the time, it would happen. You read about that sort of thing all the time. So put it out of your head.'

'Do you?' Aisling hadn't read about it.

'Well, no, but I'm sure I've read it somewhere. You know the sorta thing where people think they can't have a baby, so they adopt and then voila, they get pregnant once the stress of trying is out of the equation.'

Aisling bit her lip to stop herself from snapping. Life according to Leila. Give her strength. She'd not been on the hormone tablets long, but already she was quick to fire, although she wasn't sure if that was down to the tablets or her current frame of mind. Leila meant well, and she thought she was being helpful, but she absolutely fecking well wasn't. It wasn't her fault, though, because until you'd experienced trying to get pregnant for yourself, you couldn't possibly understand.

It was easy for Leila to tell her to put it out of her mind, but it was nigh impossible to stop thinking of something simply because you knew you should. Or, at least it was for her. Even when she was busy downstairs with guests, Aisling was constantly wondering if her sore boobs meant she was pregnant or due on or whether she was weeing more than usual or feeling more tired. She couldn't help it, and she had tried to concentrate on other things.

What terrified Aisling the most was that some people had years and years of this. She'd no clue how they coped. She was doing her best to be positive too because she knew there was a lot to be optimistic about. Her tubes were fine. Quinn's little swimmers were fine. Everything would be fine. 'Everything will be fine.'

'What was that?'

'Nothing.'

'Did you hear what I was saying about putting it out of your head?'

'Mmm,' Aisling replied, deciding evasiveness was her best form of response. It would be wise to move off the topic too, if she didn't want to fall out with her friend. 'So, go on then, you were telling me about yer woman who wants Enya to sing at her wedding?'

'She's not available, obvs,' Leila said, her tone clipped. 'Listen, I'd better run. I'm meeting Bearach for lunch.' Leila had wanted to tell her friend she was going for Sunday lunch at his parents' house and how desperate she was to make the right sort of impression on them. She'd thought they might mull over what should she wear to strike the right note like they would have in the not so distant past. It would have fallen on deaf ears, though, because all Aisling thought about and talked about was getting pregnant. She was obsessed with having a baby.

They said their goodbyes with faux joviality and as Aisling disconnected the call, her eyes burned and a lump formed in her throat. Leila was annoyed with her. Aisling couldn't recall her ever being properly annoyed with her before. But, worst of all, she didn't blame her. 'You're turning into a pregnancy bore, Aisling O'Mara-Moran,' she said to the empty room. It was true. She was becoming the sorta person who didn't listen to anyone else because she was so caught up in herself. 'Selfish is what you are,' she muttered, her hand reaching for the Snowballs. 'Selfish, selfish, selfish.' She'd stuffed two in at once, one for each cheek, when she winced. The front door had banged shut, startling her, and she'd bitten her tongue.

'It's only me, Ash,' Quinn called out.

What was he doing home? she wondered, chewing frantically and swallowing a gooey mass of marshmallow as Quinn breezed in looking pleased with himself, then, seeing no one else was in the living room, asked, 'Who were you talking to just then?'

Aisling flushed. 'Leila.' She gestured to the phone. A half-truth. He didn't need to know she'd been telling herself off. 'What are you doing home?' Aisling echoed her thoughts of a second before, straightening in her seat. She cast a guilty glance at the packet of Snowballs. Quinn knew her well enough to know they were her number one go-to, wallowing treat.

'I've come to whisk you away for the afternoon.'

'What about the restaurant?' Aisling's eyes flitted over the shirt she'd slopped tea down the front of and her chocolate stained Mo-pants. She didn't know that she wanted to be whisked away. On the contrary, she quite fancied the idea of not moving from the sofa for the foreseeable future.

'That's why we have a sous-chef, Ash, so as you, my beautiful wife, can go on a mystery date with your husband. So come on. Up and off that sofa with you, woman!'

'Do I have to get up?'

'You do.'

'Where are we going?' Aisling didn't move.

'I said 'mystery date'. If I told you, then it wouldn't be a mystery anymore.'

That was true but hardly acceptable. She couldn't rock up to a posh restaurant in her dirty Mo-pants and stained shirt. 'But what should I wear? You'll have to give me a clue.'

'Ah sure, you're grand as you are.'

Aisling frowned. She wasn't sure she liked the sound of a mystery date if they were going somewhere where her current state of clothing was deemed an acceptable standard of dress. 'Casual then?'

'Definitely casual.' She didn't want to rain on Quinn's parade, not when he was clearly geared up for whatever it was he had in store for her.

'Give me five minutes to change.'

'Ash, you really don't need to—'

'Five minutes, Quinn.' Aisling mustered up the necessary energy to retreat to their bedroom and changed into a clean blouse and her jeans before applying lipstick and fluffing her hair. That would have to do, she decided, frowning into the mirror for a final once over. Then realising she was still barefoot, she flicked her eyes across her racks of shoes settling on the Dior slingbacks.

She tottered into the living room, injecting enthusiasm into her voice. 'I'm ready.' It was lovely of Quinn to try and cheer her up, but spontaneity was overrated in her book, and she looked longingly at the sofa.

Quinn grinned, then, looking down at her feet, said, 'You might want to change those.'

'What?'

'Your shoes.'

'But I always wear heels, and besides, these aren't that high.' She lifted her foot to inspect the summery slingbacks.

'Well, just for this afternoon, do you think you could dig out a pair of trainers?'

'Trainers?' Aisling was aghast. Where on earth was he planning on taking her?

Chapter Twenty

Aisling stared at her husband as he straddled the tandem bicycle, both feet planted on the ground waiting for her to hop on the back.

He'd lost the plot if he thought she was clambering on the back of that. 'Quinn, I've not been on a bike since I was twelve,' she said, taking a backwards step. The itch in the crook of her arm intensified. It had begun itching the moment she'd seen the gates to Phoenix Park. Red-faced, sweaty, cross country memories had been triggered, and now she scratched at it furiously.

The penny had dropped as to what her husband had in mind for their mystery date soon after he'd parked near the gates of Phoenix Park. She'd watched him bounce off in the direction of the bike hire kiosk and had known precisely why her precious Dior slingbacks wouldn't have been a good idea.

Ah, Ash, there's nothing to it,' Quinn said in response to her statement of not having been on a bike in years. Then, he began warbling the Daisy Bell/Bicycle Made for Two tune.

Aisling couldn't help but smile because her husband couldn't hold a tune to save himself.

Sensing weakness, Quinn pounced, giving her a lewd wink followed by, 'C'mon now, girl, throw your leg over.'

'Be it on your head if I come off the fecking thing, Quinn Moran,' she said, clambering on. She put one gleaming white, trainer-clad foot on the pedal she was to push off on, keeping the other firmly on the asphalt.

Quinn waved the map he'd been handed when he'd hired the tandem. 'Do you want to be in charge of this, or shall I keep hold of it?'

'Sure, we'll only be going for a little pedal up the cycle path there and back, won't we. So what do we need a map for?'

Quinn twisted around, holding the paper up to show her the circled loop he had in mind. 'I thought we could stop at Farmleigh for a gander. Not a guided tour of the house as such but you know, to see how the other half used to live. Then we could see if we can spot some deer over there by the Papal Cross. What do you think if we finish where we start with a spot of afternoon tea at the Victorian Tea Rooms?' He looked thoroughly pleased with the plan.

Aisling, however, was not impressed, although she did like the sound of the afternoon tea part. 'You do know the park covers fifteen acres, don't you?' She knew this because she'd recommended a tandem bicycle ride around Phoenix Park to their more active guests over the years. Suffice to say, it hadn't been on her bucket list.

The thing Quinn was forgetting was that she wasn't an exercise sort of a girl. Not unless you counted the salsa dance lessons they'd taken or her breaking her moves out at Quinn's on the odd rowdy Saturday night. The last serious exercise she'd undertaken was when Moira had taken it upon herself to act as her and Bronagh's personal trainer in the lead up to her and Quinn's wedding. She'd had them both charging up and down the stairs of the guesthouse, determined to get them in shape for Aisling's big day.

A nightmare about summed that up.

'Two young fit Dubliners like ourselves, Ash? Sure it will be a doddle,' Quinn stated.

'Speak for yourself,' Aisling grumbled.

Quinn either didn't hear her or decided to ignore her because he announced, 'Right, are you ready? We'll set off on the count of three.'

Aisling opened her mouth to reply, but he was already doing the countdown, and before she knew it, they were off.

It was a wobbly start, and a few heads turned as Aisling shrieked, but the old saying was true she mused five minutes into it. You really didn't forget how to ride a bike. Her shoulders loosened and her vicelike grip on the handlebars relaxed. She even kicked her legs out either side like you saw people doing in the films as they sailed past the Wellington Monument and approached Dublin Zoo.

The wind was in her hair, the sun was shining, and she was on a date with the man she loved. Life was good, Aisling thought, sighing happily. She'd left all her worries behind and was filled with the urge to burst into song —'Born Free' sprang to mind. But then a squirrel darted out in front of them and shot up a nearby tree and the moment was gone as Quinn suddenly swerved. There was a precarious second where she wasn't sure they'd stay upright, but he managed to steady the bicycle, and they carried on their way.

Cars puttered past the road running alongside the path they were following, as did the green Hop-on Hop-off sightseeing bus. They waved up at the tourists sitting on the open top with their cameras at the ready.

'Keep left,' Quinn ordered as though he were an authority on the rules of road cycling as they approached those on foot.

Couples with the same idea as Quinn waved out as they biked past on the opposite side of the road. Aisling waved back enthusiastically in an aren't we grand out on tandems like so, way.

A steady trail of families was entering and exiting the zoo, and Aisling recalled childhood visits of her own. The highlight had been the ice cream she knew she'd be after getting at some point in the afternoon. Most of her memories were food-related, she mused, thinking it was written in the stars she'd marry a chef.

'Aisling, you are pedalling, aren't you?'

'The pedals are going around, aren't they?' she replied indignantly.

Quinn angled his head so his voice wouldn't get lost on the breeze beginning to whip up. 'I know that but are you actually pushing them around, or are you resting your feet on the pedals while I do all the pushing?'

'My legs are doing plenty of hard graft, thank you very much.' She'd realised as to why she'd thought this cycling lark was a walk in the park, so to speak and decided she'd better give it some welly.

Quinn flapped the map he was still holding. 'At the next roundabout, we hang a left.' The bike veered towards the kerb and Aisling wished he'd keep both his hands on the handlebars.

True to his word, he stuck his arm out to indicate the manoeuvre as they turned left and pedalled past a woodland copse. Aisling risked a glance skyward as the warmth of the sun went behind a cloud.

'What's the forecast for this afternoon?' she shouted.

'I dunno.'

Aisling's mouth tightened. How could he call himself Irish? The first thing you did when planning an outdoor excursion was to check the weather. She didn't like the look of that cloud.

'Don't we turn up there?' Aisling shouted once more as they carried on past the path she was pointing to.

'No, sure, I checked the map. Leave the directions to me.'

The driveway to the Ordnance Survey buildings loomed.

'I'm sure we've gone too far.' Aisling's legs were getting tired.

'Aisling, I know how to read a map.'

Ten minutes later, the complicated business of performing a three-point turn on a tandem bicycle was undertaken as they pedalled back from where they'd come. This time they took the right turn off with Aisling mouthing 'told you so' at the back of Quinn's head as the Edwardian manor house came into view. A shroud of purple wisteria flowers added a splash of colour to the Greek-columned entrance.

'It's very grand, so,' Quinn said, braking short of the sweep of drive at the front of the building. 'It's used for functions and visiting dignitaries and the like nowadays, isn't it?'

'According to the brochure we've got in the lobby, yer Guinness fellow married his cousin like they did back in the day and had it built. Eventually, it was sold to the Irish government by the Guinness family.'

'I'm glad I married you and not one of my cousins,' Quinn said, twisting around to grin at Aisling. 'They've all heads on them like busted cabbages.'

Aisling laughed and then shivered. Why hadn't she brought a cardigan? That wind was getting a bite to it. 'Let's carry on, shall we?' She'd warm up once they were moving again.

It wasn't long before they were cycling along the path running parallel to the main road through the park, and this time they couldn't miss the turnoff to the Papal Cross.

'Hard right at the Phoenix Park monument,' Quinn bossed.

The simple white metal cross stood one hundred and sixteen feet high and marked where Pope John Paul II had celebrated Mass in 1979. It was what she saw beyond it that had Aisling give a soft cry of delight, though; a herd of fallow deer frolicking on the grassy expanse stretching far and wide. Quinn braked smoothly, and they both clambered off the tandem, propping the bike up with its stand before wandering past the monument. They sat down a short distance away from the deer, who were unperturbed by human presence.

'They're sweet,' Aisling murmured, smiling at the smaller of the herd's playful antics. She plucked at the grass next to her before leaning into Quinn. His arm settled around her shoulder. She was feeling contented but started as Quinn exclaimed, 'Ah, Jaysus! Would you look at those eejits over there feeding the baby ones!'

Aisling spied a family happily tossing picnic scraps to the smaller of the herd. 'Eejits,' she agreed. She didn't know much about Dublin's resident deer, but she did know feeding them was a no-no. Her attention was caught and held by a majestic stag on the edge of the group. 'Look at yer wan over there with the big horns.'

'Antlers, Ash.'

She fidgeted, feeling the buck's eyes boring into her. His ears had flattened, so they were sticking out at right angles on either side of his head. 'Is he looking at us, do you think?' She squinted into the sun, which was valiantly warding off the dark clouds. 'He's definitely giving me a look Quinn,' she added nervously.

'No, he's not. Sure, he'll be far too busy checking out the deer to pay us any mind. The mating season starts in October. He'll be taking notes on his favourites.'

'You know a lot about it.' Aisling eyed her husband curiously.

He grinned. 'School project.'

'Fair play.' She scuttled backwards a split-second later, not convinced her husband was the David Attenborough of the deer world he was purporting to be. 'He's definitely looking at us,' Aisling said. 'I don't like it.'

Quinn put his hand up to his eyes like a visor. 'He does seem to be.' He side-eyed his wife. 'Your hair's a similar colour to the does over there. I dunno maybe he's confused?'

'Thanks very much.' Alarm crept into Aisling's voice. 'Why's he flattening his ears back and putting his horns, I mean, antlers down like so?'

'Erm, I don't know.' Quinn was hesitant. 'I think he might be getting ready for the rut.'

'Jaysus feck, Quinn, he's coming toward us.'

They both scrambled to their feet.

'Back away slowly, Aisling. Don't give him any cause to get any more excited than he already is. He might think I'm the competition. You know another buck trying to steal the doe he's got his eye on.'

If Aisling hadn't been terrified, she might have found her husband alluding to being a young buck amusing, but the stag had taken another step in their direction, and sod not running!

They legged it over to the bike, hauling it upright and clambering on in record speed. Their legs spun around like the clappers as they took off down the path back towards the road. Aisling swivelled around, half expecting to see an excited stag galloping, or whatever it was deer did, towards them, but mercifully the coast was clear.

'My heart's pounding, so it is,' she said when they slowed their pace, having decided they were a safe enough distance away.

'So's mine,' Quinn shouted back. 'We'll laugh about what just happened one day, you know.'

A fat drop of rain plopped on Aisling's head. 'It's starting to rain,' she stated.

'Are you sure? I haven't felt anything.'

The heavens opened right at that moment.

'C'mon, we're on the home run!' Quinn yelled as they rode into a headwind with driving rain.

Aisling's legs were killing her by the time they reached the Victorian Tea Rooms. It might be pouring down and drenched she may well be, but she was not forfeiting her afternoon tea, she told Quinn. He'd suggested they go home, given how soaked they were.

They parked the bike under a tree for shelter and made their way bowlegged inside the quaint old building. It resembled a bandstand with a red tile roof plonked on top of it, Aisling thought. The interior was cosy and welcoming. There was an olde worlde theme to fixtures and fittings befitting its name.

The specials were scrawled on a blackboard, and the food cabinet had been depleted given the time of day but, Aisling's heart leapt, there was a lonely piece of cheesecake left waiting to be loved. 'I'll have the cheesecake,' she jumped in before Quinn could put dibs on it. He knew better than to suggest sharing, so he ordered a slice of apple pie and two coffees from the young girl serving behind the counter.

Aisling plonked down at a table and gazed out of the windows which encircled the building. The rain was still coming steadily down. Quinn pulled out a chair and sat down opposite her. She dragged her eyes away from the gloomy vista and took stock of his downcast expression.

'What's wrong? Was there no cream to be had with the apple pie?'

He mustered up a smile. 'There was cream alright, or there'd be murder. It's just, well, look at you all wet like.'

'I'll dry, and I don't mind being wet if there's cheesecake.' She waited to see if he'd raise a smile. 'That's more like it,' she said as she was rewarded with a slight grin.

'I'm sorry it all went to custard today. I wanted to do something romantic, and Paula said the most romantic date she'd ever been on was a tandem bike ride through Phoenix Park. I didn't think we'd wind up getting chased by a randy stag and drenched in a downpour.'

Paula was a waitress at Quinn's. As Aisling sat there, water pooling on the floor beneath her chair, she made a note to remember to thank her for planting the idea in her husband's head. For the first time in a long while, Aisling had been right there in the moment with Quinn. Not once that afternoon had she thought about her quest to get pregnant. Their outing had been the tonic she'd needed.

Now, she sniggered at the memory of the look on Quinn's face when he'd suggest the stag might have mistaken him for a buck and her for a doe.

'What?'

'I was thinking about your expression when that stag began to advance.'

'It wasn't funny, Ash. We could have found ourselves on the end of those antlers.'

'It is sorta funny, you know,' Aisling cajoled. 'I think he thinks you're a doe, and I'm a buck,' she mimicked.

Quinn's mouth twitched, 'Yeah, I suppose it is.'

She leaned forward in her seat and put her hand on top of his. 'And for the record, I've had a grand afternoon.'

She took her hand back as their food was brought over.

'Your coffees won't be long,' the girl said, smiling at them both. 'Jaysus, you're sodden. Do you want me to see if I can find youse a towel to dry off with?'

'Ah no, we'll be fine, and thanks a million, this looks delicious.' Aisling slid her cheesecake with its berry coulis closer and picked up her fork.

'Enjoy,' the girl said, disappearing off to make their hot drinks.

Aisling dug into her dessert. 'Mmm, there is one thing that would make up for getting soaked in the rain and stalked by a deer.'

'What's that then?' Quinn asked, his fork full of pie crust and cream hovering halfway between his mouth and the plate.

'Some of that cream.'

Quinn plopped a heaped teaspoonful onto her plate in a show of true, selfless husbandly love.

Chapter Twenty-one

'Ita, how're you?' Chris boomed cheerily, his voice bouncing off the church hall walls.

Ita was physically fine. But knowing the choirmaster's enthusiastic greeting was because he expected good news made her feel sick. Chris wanted to hear the problem of who would play the piano in Lisdoonvarna had been solved thanks to Ita's mam.

She forced a smile. 'Grand thanks, Chris, yourself?'

'Oh, I can't complain.' He waited while she discarded her bag and dropped the light jacket she'd pulled on as an afterthought before leaving the house.

Ita had pleaded one last time with her mam, who'd been ensconced on the sofa ready for her night's tele viewing, a cup of tea and biscuits at the ready, but her answer hadn't changed. It was still a big fat no.

Ita wanted to cry with the frustration of it all. Why couldn't her mam do this one thing for her and help herself at the same time? Not that she knew why Ita was so desperate for her to come to Lisdoonvarna. Now, however, her refusal made the possibility of things ever changing for Kate Finnegan seem more remote than ever.

'Dare I ask how you got on with your mam?' Chris, tired of waiting, came right out with it.

He'd had a haircut, Ita noticed idly. His thatch of silver hair was shorter than usual. It made him look younger. This hadn't escaped Angela's notice because she was hovering, waiting to pounce.

Ita opened her mouth, intent on telling him they'd have to find somebody else to stand in for Breda but what popped forth instead was, 'She's delighted to have been asked.' This was the complete opposite of what had transpired when she'd broached the trip with her mam, and she couldn't believe she'd said it.

'That's good news altogether!' Chris clapped his hands. Ita, could you tell Mrs Finnegan we're equally delighted she'll be joining us?' There was a murmuring consensus from those milling about waiting for the rest of the Gaelic and Raw choir members to show.

'I will, and it's Kate. My mam says being called Mrs Finnegan makes her feel old.' She couldn't look Chris in the eye, and leaving him at the mercy of Angela, she mooched over to join Oisin and Mags.

'Oh, and Ita?'

'Yes?'

'Perhaps she could join us on Friday? Then Breda could run through the songs for the festival performances with her.'

'I'll mention it.'

Chris nodded and bent to retrieve the sheet music for the night's rehearsal, but Angela had other ideas. Ita overheard her asking the poor man to listen as to whether her pitch was right. She winced as Angela did the vocal equivalent of a wedgie by launching straight into the tricky high notes of 'Sweet Child O' Mine'.

'Jaysus, she'd give you the earache that one. That's grand about your mammy, Ita.' Mags grinned. The faux diamond stud in her nose caught the light. Tonight's full-skirted, rock 'n' roll style dress was eye-popping blue with polka dots. 'I'm counting down the sleeps now until we go. Zeb can't wait either.' She pulled a face and laughed, 'I'm not sure how I feel about that.'

Ita's evasive mmm in response to Mags didn't escape Oisin's notice, but she was oblivious to his thoughtful gaze as he looked at her from under his too-long fringe. Her mind had drifted elsewhere.

She'd put her plan to get her unsuspecting mother tagging along to Lisdoonvarna as a stand-in pianist into action on Sunday morning. Sunday mornings meant Kate

Finnegan would be off to Mass later and Ita wanted to soften her up with breakfast in bed.

First things first, she'd cuddled and fed Snuffy. The tabby had been mewling as though he'd been abandoned for a month. Then she flicked the kettle on.

Ita went through the motions of making breakfast, popping it all on a tray to carry upstairs.

Her hands shook a little as she carried it upstairs and the tea sloshed in the mug but didn't spill. She took a deep breath to steady herself. Still, it didn't stop the anxiety over what her mother would say to the idea of Lisdoonvarna. Ita was hoping the element of surprise would sway her, or she'd agree to go while half asleep.

The knock on the door woke Kate out of a pleasant dream she was having. Her boss, miserly auld Mr Byrne, had seen the error of his ways and was bestowing a generous Christmas bonus upon her.

Her eyes blinked open, and she lay there wondering if she'd dreamt the sound.

'Morning, Mam,' Ita sang out, stepping into the bedroom. She could smell a sweet perfume and saw the window was open a crack. The wall outside was covered in a pink climbing rose that was a riot of pink blooms. Her mam had given up on lots of things after her father had left, but maintaining a garden hadn't been one of them. These days they might only have a small strip of lawn out the back, but the grass looked as if it had been snipped with nail scissors and the clusters of pot plants were bountiful with pansies and gardenia.

Kate blinked again as she pulled herself from sleep. Her hair was darker than Ita's, but that was because she coloured it these days. She wore it to her shoulders in the same style she'd always worn it. Her daughter shared the same green cat's eyes as her and a wide mouth. Unfortunately, like Ita, her face in repose gave off a dissatisfied air.

'Sit up, Mam,' Ita bossed.

Kate hauled herself upright, placing another pillow behind her back before fumbling for her glasses on the bedside table. Catherine Alliott's latest novel was splayed open next to them. Once she'd her glasses on, Ita placed the tray down on her lap.

'What's all this in aid of, Ita?' Kate asked bewilderedly.

'Can't a daughter do something nice for her mam because she wants to?'

Kate's eyes narrowed behind the lenses, 'You didn't take the car again and prang it, did you? Christ on a bike, Ita you know you're not on the insurance.'

'Mam! Calm down. It's tea, toast, and a soft boiled egg, that's all. I haven't done anything.'

Kate didn't look convinced, and Ita knew it was now or never. She sat down at the foot of the bed. 'Mam, there is something.'

Kate put down the mug she'd only just picked up. 'I knew it.'

'It's nothing bad. Gaelic and Raw are booked to play at a festival in Lisdoonvarna in mid-September, and our pianist has pulled out.'

'You never mentioned you were going away.' Kate tried to keep the accusatory note from her voice. She knew she put too much on Ita, but if anyone was to blame for that, then it was Gerard.

'Mam, I don't have to tell you all the ins and outs of my life. I'm not a child.' Ita's tone was sharper than she'd intended, and she swallowed hard.

'I never said you were.' Kate snapped, tapping the top of the egg more vigorously than was necessary with the back of her teaspoon. 'Is it the matchmaking festival you're after going to?'

Ita nodded.

'A load of old rubbish, that is.' Kate removed the top and picked up a toast soldier, plunging it into the egg. The golden yolk oozed over the side of the eggshell.

'Dippy but not overly runny, how you like it,' Ita announced, hoping they could get back on track.

Kate gave an appreciative murmur then spoiled it by saying, 'So why does a mad festival in the boondocks warrant breakfast in bed.'

Ita replied in a desperate gush, 'We need a pianist, Mam. Breda normally plays, but her husband has a hospital appointment scheduled, and she can't come. It's too short a notice to advertise for someone, and if we don't find a stand-in, then we won't be able to go.'

Kate chewed then swallowed what was left of her soldier. 'And you want me to step in? But I haven't played in years, Ita, you know that. So what on earth made you think of me?'

'Ah, Mam, sure, you'd be grand once you sat down in front of the piano. It would all come back to you, so. You know it would. Think of it as a free holiday. You're always saying you could do with a break. The coach and accommodation are all paid for by the festival organisers. All you'd have to do is bang out a few tunes.'

Kate fixed her daughter with a hard stare. 'No, Ita.'

Ita wasn't giving up. 'But, Mam, we, I need you to come.' She pleaded with her eyes as well.

'I said no, and I meant it.' Kate held her hand up the way she used to when Ita was a child, and she'd overstepped the mark.

There was no point pushing it. Ita knew the look on her mam's face all too well. The bed creaked as she stood up. She paused to look at her as she nibbled another sliver of toast. 'Just once, Mam, I wish you'd think of someone other than yourself.'

Kate put the teaspoon down and watched as Ita stomped from the room. She jumped as her bedroom door was banged shut and glanced down at the half-eaten breakfast. Her appetite had deserted her and picking up the tray, she put it on the far side of the bed.

'Earth to Ita.' Mags was waving her hand in front of her face.

Ita blinked. "Wha—oh sorry.' She let Mags pull her into place between her and Oisin in the choir line-up. A whiff of something crisp that made her think of the colour blue tickled her nose. Oisin didn't usually wear aftershave, she thought. Whatever it was, though, it was nice and had, for a split-second, taken her mind off the fib she'd told.

The rehearsal passed in a blur, with Ita barely aware she was even singing. Before she knew it, she was shrugging her jacket back on and calling out goodbyes to those already on their way from the hall.

She needed to tell Chris the truth, but how? Especially given she'd told him Kate would be going in front of everyone. She was such an eejit.

'Ita,' Chris called as she slunk from the hall, unable to bring herself to come clean. 'Don't forget to tell Mrs Finnegan, erm Kate was it?'

Ita turned and nodded, trying not to look too miserable.

'How delighted we are she's coming.'

'I won't.' She nearly ran out of the door.

Outside, a soft, barely noticeable rain had begun to fall. No one was keen on a pint tonight, having decided to leave it until Friday. The sound of motors starting and goodnights being called filled the air. Mags was already out on the street, unlocking the door of the rusty old hatchback she drove. She waved over and called out, 'See you Friday!' Ita gave her a half-hearted wave back and started down the path to the gate, jumping as she heard Oisin's voice behind her.

'Wait up, Ita.'

'I thought you'd left already,' she said, spinning around.

He shook his head and pushed his hair out of his eyes. It promptly fell back into place, and he gave up, shoving his hands in the pocket of his suede jacket. The rock band on his shirt tonight was Alice in Chains, she noticed.

'No, I hung back because I wanted to talk to you.'

'Oh?'

'We can walk and talk. I'll see you home if you like?'

'But you live the other way.' Ita was puzzled as to what was going on. Their feet crunched over the pebbled path to the gate, and she waited for him to explain, watching as he unlatched the gate.

'It's no bother. You're not far, are you?'

'No, it's a ten-minute walk.' She began walking briskly, acutely aware her hair was frizzing in the drizzle. He fell into step alongside her, his lanky legs easily keeping pace with her.

'So what did you want to talk about?' she asked, curiosity clawing at her.

'Your mam didn't say yes to playing the piano, did she?'

'What do you mean?' Her head swivelled up to look at him. She hadn't expected that.

'Just what I said.'

His eyes were serious behind his glasses and her face heated up. There was no point in lying. She could tell he knew the answer anyway, and looking away, she said, 'She flat out refused, and I don't know why I fibbed to Chris. It came out like, and then it was too late to take it back without looking like an eejit in front of everyone.' Her voice wobbled as a lump formed in her throat. She swallowed hard, not wanting to cry in front of Oisin and look like even more of an eejit. 'I don't know what to do. I can't let everybody down. I thought it was the perfect excuse to get Mam to Lisdoonvarna, but I should have known she'd dig her heels in and say no.'

He reached out and touched her arm gently. 'You really believe that stuff about the matchmaker and his book, don't you?'

Ita fixated on the pavement and nodded. 'I have to,' she mumbled. All the worry over her future and her mam's welled up then. 'I don't know how I can ever leave her and have a life of my own while she's miserable. Who'd look after her?' she blurted. 'And I'm terrified of winding up like her bitter and alone.'

'She's not your responsibility, though, Ita. You're not responsible for making her happy. You've your own life to lead.'

'I know that. I do, but...' Her voice wobbled with threatened tears that had sprung from nowhere, and she broke off.

'Hey, don't get upset.'

Ita risked a glance up at him and saw no judgement on his face. It broke the dam, and to her utter embarrassment, she couldn't stop the fat tears that had welled from spilling over.

Oisin stopped, and his arms moved awkwardly as he hesitated for a moment before pulling her into an awkward embrace.

It was nice. Oisin was nice. Ita thought, leaning her head into his solid chest for a brief second. Still, she didn't want him to feel sorry for her. 'I'm sorry,' she mumbled, pulling away, embarrassed by her dramatic outburst.

'Don't be. I've three sisters.'

They carried on walking.

'Maybe I could talk to her?'

'You?'

They'd reached the busy intersection, and Oisin pressed the button and laughed.

'Don't look so horrified. I can be quite persuasive when I want to be, you know. I was into debating at high school.'

She wanted to say, But you always seem so quiet, but she didn't. It was difficult to picture the quiet, bookish Oisin as a self-assured debater.

They stood in silence, waiting for the signal to cross the road.

Ita mulled his offer over and decided she had nothing to lose. The last of her tears were swiped away as she said, 'Well, you can try, but I'm warning you she's not easy, so I'm not expecting a miracle.'

Chapter Twenty-two

Ita prayed that in the two hours she'd been away at choir practice, her mam hadn't decided to don her nightwear.

Kate was apt to take herself off upstairs as early as eight o'clock some nights, putting her nighty and gown on during the television adverts. She'd reappear with her face devoid of the light makeup worn for work going on about how she might as well get comfortable given she was settling in for the night.

This wasn't usually an issue because Ita didn't care if her mam was in her slippers and dressing gown while it was still light outside. Sure it was no skin off her nose. Tonight was different, though. She was conscious of Oisin standing behind her as the key turned in the lock, and she pushed the door open. If her mam was sat on her chair in her favourite Marks and Sparks nightgown, she'd be mortified.

'Mam, it's me. I've a friend with me,' she shouted out an advance warning as she stepped into the narrow hall. Hopefully, she'd have time to at least do her gown up, Ita thought. The sight of her mother in her pink cotton summer nighty braless was not one she wanted Oisin, or anyone for that matter, to be greeted with.

'Should I take my shoes off?' Oisin asked, checking his soles on the front doorstep.

Ita saw a shadow streak around the kitchen door as she flicked on the hallway light. It was followed by the slap of the cat door opening and then closing. Poor old Snuffy would have been waiting patiently for her return. The tabby would be most put out that Ita had brought a stranger home.

'No, sure you're grand. Come in.'

Oisin did so, shutting the door behind him. He followed her lead into the front room off to their left, nearly walking into the back of her as Ita came to a sudden halt. She wanted to see how the land lay or rather the state of her mam before letting him venture forth.

Kate Finnegan was leaning forward in her chair with the remote in her hand. It was aimed at the television, and she promptly hit the off button. She was still dressed in the skirt and blouse she wore to work, the last vestiges of the mauve pink lipstick she favoured clinging to her lips. There were speckles of black under her eyes from her habit of picking her mascara off while watching television. The only concession to comfort was her stocking-clad feet with her shoes abandoned under the coffee table.

Ita exhaled. She was perfectly respectable, and stepping aside she allowed Oisin to enter the room. He stood alongside her.

Kate put the remote down on the chair's arm and, sitting up straight, gave them both her full attention. Her mouth parted slightly in surprise as she registered Ita's friend was male. Well, now this was a first.

'Mam, this is my friend Oisin from Gaelic and Raw. Oisin this is my mam, Kate Finnegan.'

'It's nice to meet you, Mrs Finnegan.' Oisin strode over to her and held out his hand.

'Kate, Oisin, call me Kate.'

Ita watched as they shook hands. Subtly was not one of her mother's strong suits, and it made her squirm seeing her size Oisin up as she gave him the head to toe once over. What was running through her head, she wondered, trying to see him through her mam's eyes.

For her part, Kate was feeling relieved because she'd been about to scoot upstairs to throw her nighty on. The crime drama she was in the midst of only had fifteen minutes left to run, and she hadn't wanted to miss the end. She couldn't remember the name of the programme, but it was edge of yer seat stuff. However, the sight of Ita with a young man was one that nearly had her falling off her chair!

Her eyes grazed over his scuffed trainers and carried on upwards, getting the measure of him. His tee shirt depicted a band of ruffians, the sort who'd scream not sing. His jacket harked back to the seventies and was thrift store through and through, and she thought as her eyes settled on his face, he could have benefitted from a trim.

All that aside, however, he'd honest eyes with a smile that reached them. That said a lot about a person that did. He was cleanly shaven too, and the hand she'd shaken was warm and dry with no hint of cheating, fibber's sweaty palm. The fact he smelled of something fresh and crisp, too, hadn't escaped her notice.

This was a blessing because not all young men practised good hygiene, something she'd experienced in the queue at Tesco this very lunchtime. She'd been stuck behind a lad around the same age as this Oisin. Unlike Oisin here, though, his hair was in desperate need of a wash, and worse was the stink of BO coming off him. It had almost been enough to make her put the prawn and mayo sandwich she had in her hands back. Almost. Yes, she decided, having finished her inventory, all things considered, Ita could do a lot worse.

'Have a seat, why don't you, Oisin. Come and make yourself at home.' She beamed up at him in a proper welcome and waved to the two-seater sofa on the right of her armchair that Ita usually commandeered.

'Thank you, Kate.' He duly sat down, resting his hands, palms down, on his thighs and angling his body toward her.

It was odd to see a man sitting in her front room, Kate thought, realising Ita, who'd been off- hand with her earlier, was fidgeting about like an eejit. 'Go and put the kettle on and make us a pot of tea, Ita. There are chocolate digestives hidden behind the tins in the cupboard too. You don't want your young man here to die of thirst, now do you?' She didn't wait for Ita's response, turning to Oisin, 'I have to hide the chocolate biscuits, or there'd be none left for visitors.'

Ita hurried off, blushing furiously at her mam, referring to Oisin as her young man. Even worse, she'd made her sound like a proper piggy Peggy who couldn't control herself around the chocolate biscuits. It was true enough, but the part about saving them for visitors wasn't. What visitors? She shuddered, turning the light on in the kitchen. God only knew what her mam would say to him while she was making the tea. It was tempting to creep back down the hall to earwig while she waited for the kettle to come to the boil.

Ita was about to do that when Snuffy poked his head in through the cat door giving a plaintive meow. 'C'mon, boy. It's only Oisin. He won't hurt you. I promise.'

The cat pushed through the flap, and she picked him up, cuddling him close for a moment or two. His rumbly purr made her feel happy. 'Now, don't be silly and go running off. You're fine, so you are.' She put him down to pour the water over the teabags in the pot, and with a swish of his tail, he mooched off to sit under the table.

Ita carried the tray through to the front room with trepidation. Her mam probably had all her old school photos out by now. Jaysus, she'd die if she showed him the one where her mam had insisted on giving her hair a cut the night before class photos. She'd cut it too short, and she'd looked like a moon-faced eight-year-old there in the front row. She nudged the door open with her foot, shooting Oisin a wary smile as he shifted to look at her. His grin was comforting, but the sight of her mam with her head tilted back as she laughed at whatever he'd been saying, properly laughed, took Ita by surprise. She should laugh more often, she decided, setting the tray down. It took ten years off her.

'Oisin was after telling me the funniest story,' Kate said, wiping at her eyes. 'About your choir group. Ita never tells me anything about it you know other than "it was fine".'

Ita raised an eyebrow as she knelt down on the floor and set out the good china cups on their saucers. The only reason she never elaborated was that her mam never seemed interested. It was a cursory question tossed at her when she returned home from practice. Her eyes never strayed from the television, and she'd never pushed for more.

'I was after telling Kate about Angela's and Pauline's quest to hook Chris despite his wedding band.'

Ita nearly missed the cup as she poured the tea. Her mam would surely take umbrage at that given the circumstances of her own divorce. Wonders would never cease, though, because she was giggling again listening to Oisin.

'He needs a bodyguard on this tour of ours, but then again, if we can't find a replacement for Breda, we won't be going anyway. It will be such a shame what with all the extra rehearsals we've been putting in.'

Ah, Ita thought, catching his wink, that was his angle. 'How do you have your tea?' she asked him, a smile playing at the corner of her mouth.

'Milk and one sugar please,' he replied. 'Kate, Ita mentioned you play.'

It was apparent someone did. There was a piano in the front room. It took up too much space for something that was never touched.

Kate couldn't part with it for sentimental reasons, and even though Ita had never seen her dusting it, the walnut timber always had a mellow sheen.

Kate wagged a finger at Oisin playfully. 'Don't think I don't know what you're up to, young man.'

Ita plopped a sugar in Oisin's tea, stirring it a little too vigorously. Here we go, she thought. Her teeth nipped her bottom lip as she waited for her mam to tell him he was wasting his breath if he thought he could trick her into agreeing to come to the festival with them.

Oisin was unabashed. 'You've got my number there alright, Kate, and sure you can't blame a man for trying. We were so looking forward to our moment in the sun, weren't we, Ita? And now it's looking as though it's not going to happen. It's disappointing so.'

Ita nodded her agreement.

Kate got up then and smoothed her skirt. 'Well, we all need our moment in the sun,' she said crisply as she moved over to the piano.

Ita forgot all about the tea as she sat back on her haunches, eyes wide as her mam lifted the lid of the old console. There wasn't a sound in the room as Kate stared down at the keys, her expression unreadable. Then she trailed her fingers over them. The sound reverberated in the room.

'I haven't had it tuned in an age,' Kate said, fixing Oisin with an apologetic half-smile before sitting down on the red velvet-covered stool. She flexed her wrists for a moment and then began to play a scale. 'C major,' she said almost to herself, running through a few more before raising her head. 'Shall we see how rusty I am?'

Oisin, who was angled so he could see over the back of the sofa, said, 'I doubt you're rusty at all, Kate.'

Ita didn't dare say a word, not wanting to break the spell.

'Have you the sheet music for the songs you're going to be singing?' Kate asked.

Oisin and Ita both lurched towards their bags to retrieve the songbooks, but Oisin beat her to it. He passed the book to Kate, who flicked through it, frowning.

'I suppose the beginning is as good a place to start as any,' she said, placing the book open on the stand in front of her.

The piano version of 'Sweet Child O' Mine' filled the room, and Oisin and Ita glanced at one another, reading each other's minds as they began to sing along.

Oisin wailed out the ending, and the trio beamed at one another. Something magical had happened, and it wasn't just the music, Ita thought, looking at her mam's luminous face.

'What do you think? Will I do?' Kate Finnegan asked.

'You'll be grand,' Oisin grinned.

Ita couldn't wipe the smile off her face, not even when her mam said, 'Ita stop grinning gormlessly and offer the lad the chocolate biscuits.'

Chapter Twenty-three

'Mam, hurry up,' Moira called by the open front door, jangling the car keys for good measure. Then with a huff, 'I'll be in the car.'

Maureen ignored her and carried on hunting for her sunglasses. They were like socks, she mused, running a hand over the top of the fridge. They'd a mysterious habit of disappearing.

'These what you're looking for?' Donal appeared with Kiera on his hip, the errant black framed sunglasses in his hand.

They exchanged a smile that said, aren't we lucky knowing what the other's thinking.

'Where were they?'

'Where you left them, Mo, on the outside table.'

'What would I do without you?' Maureen said, pushing them up on top of her head.

'I don't know. What would she do without me, Kiera?' Donal jiggled the plump baby, and she made a grab for his beard, her current source of fascination.

Maureen leaned in and kissed her granddaughter. 'You be a good girl for Poppa D.' She left behind a raisin imprint, a new shade she wasn't sure about but which Moira said was on-trend. She planted a smacker on Donal, who didn't mind looking like Kenny Rogers with raisin coloured lips and then ordered him to wear his new sandals when he went for a walk with Kiera. 'Your toenail's beginning to clear up nicely thanks to all the fresh air it's after getting.' Their relationship was stronger, too, thanks to the cessation of the flipping and flopping about the place. The sandals bought from Carrick's were worth every penny, she thought.

Pooh sidled up alongside him, looking mournfully up at her.

'Daddy will take you too when he goes for a walk, Pooh. Won't you, Daddy?' She paused to pet the poodle, who didn't look impressed by the promise of a walk if it wasn't his beloved mistress leading the charge. Nor was he fussed about this 'daddy' business.

'Maureen, I don't think it's working. I'm convinced that's a growl he's after giving whenever you refer to me as daddy.'

'No, sure, it's his way of purring. You know like a cat.'

Donal didn't look too confident, but Pooh was like a second son to Maureen, and as such, he'd continue to try to bond with the poodle. Maureen had got it in her head the dog was feeling pushed out since Kiera's arrival and that it might make him feel more secure if they referred to Donal as Daddy.

The horn sounded.

'I'll swing for that girl. Impatient mare,' Maureen muttered, picking up her handbag and marching towards the door. She paused and turned, striking a model pose as Donal bobbed Kiera's hand up and down in a wave. 'Will I do?'

'You look lovely, Mo.'

Maureen flicked her navy scarf over her shoulder and waved back at Kiera before stepping out the door in her gleaming white pedal pushers. She'd teamed them with a red tee shirt with little stars decorating it. Moira said she looked like she was about to put her hand on her heart and begin singing 'The Star-Spangled Banner' at any moment.

'Oh, and Donal?' she tossed over her shoulder, 'don't forget to put her in the pink dress I've laid out on the changing table before you head out.'

'I won't, and I'll put the bonnet on her too.'

'Good man.' Maureen closed the door behind her.

Another toot made Maureen jump. She shot daggers at her daughter, who was tapping the steering wheel impatiently. Anyone would have thought she'd been driving for years the cockiness of her sitting there, she thought, but as she spied Amanda, her face morphed into a sunny smile. Her neighbour was rubbing her head. The sudden tooting had caused her to bang it on the boot. Three Marks & Spencer bags were at her feet.

'Tis alright, Amanda, it's my daughter after tooting,' Maureen called over. 'Honestly, the number of times she's kept me waiting over the years without a word of complaint from myself.' She shook her head, taking stock of Amanda's classy but casual shopping outfit and then glanced at the shopping bags. She should have known there'd be no shopping at Tesco's for her. 'But keep her waiting longer than two seconds, and she's her hand on the horn like so.' Maureen remembered the party. 'While I have you there, Amanda, did I happen to mention we're after deciding on a theme for the housewarming party?' She didn't wait for Amanda to reply. 'It's Hawaiian. I thought it would be a nice nod to this second summer we're after having. Hasn't the weather been glorious?'

'Mmm,' was Amanda's terse response as she bent at her knees to pick up one of the bags.

'I'll give you a hand shall I?' Maureen lunged for one of the M&S bags.

'No, thank you, Maureen.' Amanda swatted her away. 'I can manage. Best you get on your way. We don't want any more tooting now, do we?'

Maureen wasn't sure, but she thought she detected a tone from Amanda. Before she could formulate a response, however, she was distracted by her sixth sense. It was telling her Moira was about to press down on the horn once more. So she said a quick goodbye to her neighbour and crunched across the gravel to the passenger door with lightning speed and, pulling it open, stuck her head in the car. 'Don't you dare touch that horn again, Moira O'Mara or there'll be murder. You're already after getting me offside with the neighbours.'

Moira was unrepentant, gunning the engine as her mammy put one foot in the car.

'And don't even think about setting off until I've both feet in. Your father used to do that to me. Always in a hurry, he was.'

Moira decided not to push it, and her foot hovered over the accelerator, eager for the off as she waited until her mammy was buckled in. Then she put her foot down and shot down the drive, oblivious to having left Amanda coughing in a cloud of exhaust fumes.

'Too fast, Moira,' Maureen gasped as they hared onto the main road. Mercifully the street was quiet this time of the day, but still and all, Maureen decided her daughter had a heavy foot when it came to the accelerator. 'Brake, Moira, brake, you're not in the Grand Prix!' she gasped, one hand in the brace position on the dashboard as they approached a corner.

'Mammy, stop being one of those backseat drivers. I'm perfectly able. I passed my test, didn't I?'

'I'm in the front seat in case you haven't noticed, and just because you passed doesn't mean you have to be a speed demon.'

'I'm driving at the limit. We don't all drive like we're in the Popemobile cruising through the Vatican City.' Moira wrenched the steering wheel over to the right, sending her mammy lurching. 'And for your information, Donal says I'm a grand driver.'

'He's apt to take the corners too fast for my liking and all,' Maureen muttered, pushing her sunglasses, which had slid off, back into place. 'Sweet Mother of Divine, I feel like we're in that American film Thelma and Louise.'

'You're older, so you get to be Louise,' Moira supplied, her eyes never moving from the road. 'And I get to be Thelma which means it's me who does the riding with Brad Pitt in his cowboy hat.'

'Remember who it is you're sitting next to, madam.'

They reached the village without incident, but Maureen's knuckles were white, and by the time Moira managed the parallel park, a small crowd had gathered to watch. A smattering of applause sounded as she finally nudged in between the two cars and switched the engine off. Maureen unclenched her jaw as she clambered out of the car and flapped her hand at the bystanders. 'Alright, alright, you've had your fun. On your way. There's nothing to see here.'

Moira locked the car, and Maureen announced she'd call into the pirate man's café. 'I'll pick up something nice for Ciara.'

'The baby Kiera,' Christ on a bike, Mammy had her saying it now, 'I mean my Kiera?'

'No, sure, it's a café, Moira.' Maureen shook her head as though her daughter was a simpleton. 'Ciara with a 'C'. She manages the dress shop I'm taking you to. Her mammy doesn't look after her like I do you girls. So, I like to pick her up a little something to put some meat on her bones whenever I call in.'

'But what about me?'

'What about you?'

'Will you pick me up something nice too?'

'Sure, you're out with your mammy. Isn't that nice enough for you?' Maureen said, disappearing inside the café decked out in the nautical theme she was fond of since moving to Howth.

Moira loitered outside, feeling mutinous. It wasn't right her mammy buying some strange girl treats.

As it happened, Maureen picked up two of the cream slices but only because she wanted Moira in good form when she did the twirl in the dress she was planning on trying on. It was why she and Moira were out and about in the village this afternoon. Maureen wanted to get kitted out for the party, which was approaching at a rate of knots. The weeks were flying by what with one thing and another.

Appeased, Moira followed her mammy up the street. 'Is this the place then?' she asked as Maureen came to a halt.

'It is. Ciara always does me proud. It was her who introduced me to the wrap dress and the swimsuit with the control panels.'

Moira checked out the window display of the boutique Mammy was always banging on about. She recognised the dress with the red flowers draped over the mannequin from her mammy's description. It was too flowery for her liking, but sure it might look well on her mammy. She'd keep an open mind now she was back in her good books, thanks to the cream slice.

As they barrelled into the shop, Ciara, who was a waif if ever there was one, looked up from the women's magazine she was flicking through. She hastily shoved it under the counter. She'd had a talking to from Shirley, the boutique's owner, the other week about how slouching over the counter reading magazines was not the look they were trying to promote.

Moira's eyes narrowed, watching her mammy greet this Ciara wan as though she were the prodigal daughter herself.

Oh yes, she'd be telling Aisling and Rosi they'd have to watch out. There was competition for a fourth O'Mara sister who got treated to cream slices regularly.

'And this is my youngest daughter Moira, the baby Kiera with a K's mammy.'

Ciara and Moira sized one another up briefly while Maureen prattled on.

'I hope you're free on the sixteenth, Ciara, because we're after having a housewarming and Donal and I would be delighted if you could come. It's to have a Hawaiian theme which is why I've popped in to see you today. I've my eye on the dress in the window for the party.'

'Can I bring Pete, my boyfriend?' Ciara asked, stepping out from behind the counter to rifle through the racks until she found Maureen's size in the dress on display.

'The more, the merrier.'

Moira rolled her eyes, knowing there was no point saying anything because Mammy was a law unto herself.

Ciara gestured to a seat where Moira could sit while waiting for her mammy to try on the dress. 'A good choice, Maureen, what with it being a wrap style,' she said, hanging the dress up in the fitting room.

'You've taught me well, Ciara.' Maureen tittered, and Moira made a gagging noise that made both women turn around.

'Cream caught in my throat,' Moira muttered.

Maureen stepped into the cubicle, and Ciara pulled the curtain across. She and Moira ate their slices in silence, eyeing one another when they thought the other wasn't looking.

Maureen stripped down to her underwear and slipped into the dress, knotting it at the side. The skirt floated dreamily around her legs, and she appraised herself in the mirror, pleased. It fit her like a dream if she held her breath in. There'd be no millionaire's shortbread between now and the party. The only hesitation she had was over how low cut it was. She pursed her lips at the deep cleavage on display. Hmm, what was the saying about if you've got it, flaunt it? A new bra would have to be bought, though. One with more oomph in it. When would she find time to buy that?

The days were disappearing on her, filled as they were with all the organising. Thank goodness for her notebook or she'd lose track of what she'd done and had yet to do. There was so much to think of. The hibiscus flowers, for one. She'd managed to source them and a florist who'd make the leis for her but had heart palpations upon receiving the quote. In the end, fresh hibiscus flowers to greet their female guests had been settled on. The leis could be bought from the pound shop.

Then there'd been the menu to plan. Rosemary had come up trumps through her daughter. Maureen had placated Donal by telling him he could cook the chicken wings on the whizz-bang barbeque they'd brought home on the weekend. They were serving whole salmon and pulled pork and an array of salads with tropical fruits for dessert.

Quinn was helping her with the pork and salmon, and the girls were on the salads. Tom would be put behind the tiki bar they'd set up in the garden and from where they'd serve the fruit punch, among other drinks. Note to self, pick up some of those colourful umbrella swizzle sticks for the drinks. Yes, she thought, twisting this way and that, it was all coming together nicely. However, she was desperate to put a big red tick next to Entertainment. She was still waiting on confirmation that the girl she wanted to book to perform the hula dancing was available.

Time to get the verdict from Moira and Ciara, she thought, whipping back the curtains and flinging her arms wide, 'Ta-dah!'

Chapter Twenty-four

The Gaelic and Raw choir rumbled out of Dublin on the coach with reclining seats, and thanks be to God according to the older members of their troop a toilet, shortly after eight am. Outside their air-conditioned cocoon, the Thursday morning rush hour commute was coming to an end with the bumper to bumper stream of traffic heading into the capital thinning out.

It was a beautiful day with only a whisper of autumn in the air which added to the infectious excitement of the coach's passengers and much chatter about this second summer Ireland was in the midst of.

There'd been initial discontent as they'd neared the motorway over the reclining seats. Angela had been the most vocal protestor, declaring she'd not spend the next six hours staring at the baldy spot on the back of Bryan Geraghty's head. Everybody knew it wasn't poor Bryan's shiny scalp that had her knickers in a knot, however. Oh no, that was down to yer new woman, Kate. Ita's mam. Somehow the fill-in pianist had commandeered the prime window seat next to their Silver Fox, Chris.

Angela wasn't the only person disgruntled over the arrangement.

If Pauline had had a dolly to hand, she'd be sticking pins in it about now because she'd planned on sitting where yer interloper woman was. Oh yes, she'd visualised herself making the most of the windy patches of road they were sure to hit at some point in the journey. She'd use those sharp bends as an opportunity to accidentally, on purpose, lean into their choirmaster. But, instead, she was stuck next to Sheila Dolan, who'd enjoyed a meal the night before laced with enough garlic to ward yer vampires off for a century.

Before they'd set off, their coach driver Paddy Murphy had assured the choir group his road skills were second to none and that they were in safe hands. He'd won brownie points with the older group members when he'd said if anyone needed to visit the jacks, all they had to do was raise their hand, and he'd be sure to avoid any potholes in the road.

Paddy felt he'd drawn the short straw when he heard he'd be delivering a choir to the town of Lisdoonvarna. Sure, his friend and fellow coach driver, Declan Dooley, was charged with a coach load of folk dancers heading to the festival. At least they'd have a bit of life about them, he'd thought, fearing he was in for a six-hour road trip of mouldy old hymns. How wrong he'd been! The promise of a decent lunch stop in Athlone smoothed the fray over the reclining seats, and to his surprise, Gaelic and Raw had launched into song. Not a warbling version of 'The King of Love my Shepherd is' but rather a harmonising rendition of Journey's 'Don't Stop Believin'.

Now, this was road tripping, he thought, joining in as, taking one hand off the steering wheel, he helped himself to a mint imperial.

Ita was sitting in the window seat wondering how she'd manage the next six or so hours being overly sensitive to the proximity of Oisin's leg next to hers. Her feelings had changed for him the night he'd walked her home from choir practice. It was as if she'd taken the blinkers off because all of a sudden, he'd become incredibly attractive in her eyes. It was driving her mad.

Oisin seemed oblivious to her inner turmoil as he relaxed with his long legs stretched out under the seat in front of him. Now and then, she'd distract herself by craning her neck to see how her mam was getting on. She'd taken Oisin's suggestion that Chris could do with a bodyguard literally, it would seem, having been glued to his side from the moment they'd assembled at the Dawson Street pick-up point. She'd been having a lot of practice sessions with the choirmaster since agreeing to come to Lisdoonvarna too. Looking at her up ahead now, Ita supposed it was her way of looking out for his wife.

She still had to pinch herself as to the fact her mam was here on the bus with them. Not only that, but it was clear from the animated bobbing of her dark head and Chris's silver one, they were enjoying themselves. Ita knew she had Oisin to thank for that. She risked yet another side glance at him. He was leaning across the aisle listening to something Mags was on about.

Poor Mags had to share a room with Pauline but had refrained from making a fuss when Chris took her aside and asked her to take one for the team. He couldn't have her sharing with Angela now, could he? he'd explained. Mags had seen his point, but that didn't mean she had to like it.

Three unexpected things had happened in a short time, Ita thought, noticing the way Oisin's hair curled at the collar of his jacket. The first was her mam being here. The second was what else had happened the night he'd come back to her house and talked Kate Finnegan round.

There they'd been in the front room, her mam at the piano while she and Oisin harmonised an Anastacia number when he'd stopped singing and crouched down low. He'd begun rubbing his thumb and forefinger together. Ita wouldn't have believed what happened next if she hadn't seen it with her own two eyes. Snuffy, hesitant at first, had stalked across the room and allowed Oisin to pet him. It was unheard of, and both she and Kate, who'd stopped playing to watch, stared in amazement as the tabby lay down and rolled over to enjoy a tummy scratch. Ita had decided on the spot that not only was Oisin the mammy whisperer, but he was the cat whisperer too.

He'd looked up and seen two sets of incredulous green eyes watching him.

'Snuffy doesn't let anyone but me near him,' Ita said.

'He growls when I go near him,' Kate added.

'I love animals,' Oisin offered up. 'I suppose they sense that.'

Right then and there, Ita decided she loved Oisin.

As though feeling her eyes on him, Oisin turned questioningly to Ita, but she swung her gaze to the window and feigned interest in the patchwork fields stretching wide. A little sigh huffed from her lips.

The third unexpected thing to have happened was Oisin. She'd thought this trip to Lisdoonvarna would see her meet someone special, but he'd been under her nose all along, and she'd just not known it.

Chapter Twenty-five

Ita's breath was leaving a smudge on the window as the coach chundered past what Paddy had just informed them was Ballinalacken Castle. The imposing ruin sat atop a rocky crag, keeping watch over the roads from Lisdoonvarna to Fanore and Doolin.

It wasn't long before they'd reached the edge of the town of Lisdoonvarna itself. Paddy switched on his microphone and pointed out the Victorian looking Spa Wells complex. 'There's an alcohol-free tea dance held there between midday and two pm every day of the festival for those that abstain.'

Mags caused a snigger, remarking she wouldn't be caught dead in there.

'Sure, there's something for everybody here,' Paddy countered as the coach crawled down the main street. He carried on with his tour guide patter, informing them the little spa town where the upper classes used to come to take the waters and pair suitable marriage matches for their offspring had a population of around one thousand or so for most of the year. Come festival time, though, it could swell to as many as ten thousand. Looking at the jostling revellers outside, Ita could well believe it.

The festival was no longer solely the domain of the farmers who'd come flocking to the town to find a wife each September through to October either. Indeed, the streets thronged with people, young, old and somewhere in between. Some were dressed to the nines, and some could have not long clambered off a tractor. So many people, all come looking for love, Ita mused, feeling her excitement build as her eyes alighted on the mustard yellow Matchmaker Bar with its bright swirling mural surround.

A line of people waited to be admitted, and Ita wondered if the matchmaker man himself was in residence with his magic book. How she wished she could jump off the coach and push her way through to the front of her line to see for herself! Perhaps his book could work some magic where she and Oisin were concerned.

She cast a wistful glance at him, seeing his head was lolling to the left and his mouth was slightly open as he napped. There was no point mooning after him, she told herself. He didn't see her that way.

She distracted herself by checking out the suitable fellas for her mam. There were plenty to choose from, she noted, scanning the crowds.

Ita allowed herself a frisson of hope that the weekend would be a success where Kate was concerned but the thought of singing to numbers like this the next day filled her belly with butterflies.

An old man with a cap pulled low, and a Father Christmas beard played the fiddle outside a newsagent. A small group of revellers had gathered around him on the surrounding pavement. An older couple with their arms linked were kicking their heels up as they danced around, much to the crowds whooping and clapping delight.

Ita waved back at those waving at the passing coach, forgetting she was prone to being shy. A grin spread across her face as she spied signs with 'Marriage Material' or 'Mad for the Shift' written on them, bobbing about in the sea of people. She was itching to be out there in the midst of it all.

'And over on your left in the square is the Matchmaking Statue,' Paddy boomed.

Ita took in the bronze sculpture of a fiddler and a bodhran player performing for a couple about to waltz. A group of girls were posing next to it for a photograph and others patiently waited their turn.

The coach juddered to a stop outside a rectangular, pale lemon building with white trim. Ita craned her neck and saw the words Finney's Hotel sandwiched between the second and third-floor windows. This was it. The buildings on either side were two-storey, one a pastel pink the other a bold green. Pansies spilt over hanging baskets adorning the second storey of the pink building, a B&B, and a Guinness sign told her the green building was a pub.

Mags caught her eye across the way. 'I can't wait to get off and stretch my legs. It feels like hours since we stopped in Athlone.'

'I know. Me too.'

'I don't know how he slept through Paddy's commentary.' Mags inclined her head toward Oisin. 'Give him a nudge.'

'He was studying until late last night.' Ita repeated what Oisin had told her not long after they'd boarded the bus after lunch and he'd been unable to stop yawning. 'I'll grab forty winks now, and I'll be raring to go by the time we get there,' he'd said, shifting about trying to get comfortable.

The last hour of their journey had been a quiet one, with the initial sing-songs replaced by sporadic snores from Bryan Geraghty but not Oisin mercifully.

Now though, animated chatter was sweeping through the coach as the members of Gaelic and Raw got their second wind and clambered out of their seats, stretching as they waited to get off.

Ita saw Chris was already on his feet pulling down the leather bag he always brought along to practice from the overhead compartment. Her mam had shifted across into his seat. They were getting along famously those two, much to Ita's amazement. All eyes had been upon them as they sat together at lunch, heads close together, thick as thieves. Ita had been all set to join her mam in with herself, Mags, and Oisin but hadn't wanted to butt in and break up their tableau.

Unlike Pauline and Angela, who'd tried to muscle in on the act but finding themselves unable to get a word in edgewise, had squeezed in either side of Paddy. The fact he didn't wear a wedding ring hadn't escaped their notice.

When they got back on the bus, Oisin told her he'd nearly choked hearing Pauline say to the poor man, 'Sure, it must be a lonely life on the road for a man without a good woman to come home to.'

Paddy didn't stand a chance.

Now Ita prodded Oisin with her elbow. 'Come on. We're here.'

'What?' He straightened his head and blinked, trying to remember where he was.

'We're at the hotel in Lisdoonvarna,' Ita repeated.

He cricked his neck from side to side and then peered past her as if to confirm what she'd said. 'We're here?'

'We're here.'

'I wasn't snoring, was I?'

'No, dribbling maybe but not snoring.'

He grimaced. 'Sorry,' he said and wiped his mouth with the back of his hand. Then waiting until the coast was clear, he slid out of his seat.

Paddy already had half the coach unloaded, with luggage piled on the pavement by the time they stepped down from the coach.

Ita retrieved her bag and remembered to thank Paddy. She would have liked to have tipped him, but her budgeted funds hadn't allowed for it.

Her mam must already be in the foyer, she decided, not seeing her as she glanced about.

Mags tapped her on the shoulder. 'Meet you in the pub in twenty?' She pointed to the green building where Ita could now see the sign for O'Shea's swinging on the breeze.

'Grand.' Ita left Mags to retrieve her wheelie-case and pushed open the hotel's door. It took a moment for her eyes to adjust to the light inside. The entrance didn't have the feeling of Georgian luxury you got walking into O'Mara's, but it was quaint, she decided. There was a fireplace, not that there'd be much call for sitting on the chintz-covered sofas on either side of it this time of year, but it would be cosy in winter. She smiled as it dawned on her the shaggy grey and white Old English sheepdog sound asleep in a patch of sun by the windows wasn't a rug. She'd make friends with him later, she decided. Now, though, where was her mam?

'Ita, over here!' Kate spotted her daughter scanning the lobby and waved the key to signal she'd already checked them in.

Ita nudged past the choir members milling about, waiting to check themselves in, and joined her mam by the decrepit looking lift. It even had a grille that had to be slid across before they could step inside.

'Do you think it's safe?' Ita queried, wrestling it across. Then, finally, she stepped in and moved to the back of the lift to give her mam room with her bag.

'Only one way to find out,' Kate muttered, pressing the button for the third floor.

The lift jolted and then slowly, bone rattlingly so, climbed upwards. Not a word was spoken, but there was an audible exhale of relief from mother and daughter as they arrived on the third floor.

They checked the room numbers as they trekked down the faded carpet runner, the floorboards creaking beneath their feet.

'This is us,' Kate said, putting her bag down and unlocking the door.

Ita sent up a quick prayer for the room to be orderly so her mam would find no cause for complaint.

'Well, now this will do us nicely,' Kate said, and Ita remembered to raise her eyes heavenward and send up a quick thank you.

She took a brief inventory of the twin single beds from the doorway. The candlewick bedspreads had gone out of style in the seventies, or was it sixties? They were still a crisp white, though, and there wasn't a crease in either of them. The only other furnishings aside from the beds were a dressing table with a mirror and a small table over by the window with two chairs. It was a simple room, but it looked clean and comfortable.

Ita put her bag down on the bed closest to the window and then moved over to the window, pulling back the net curtain to see the street below. The coach was gone, she noted, wondering whether either Angela or Pauline had managed to get Paddy's telephone number before he'd disappeared off to wherever it was coach drivers went after a long journey.

She let the curtain fall and, turning around, saw her mam was already unpacking and making a strange sound. It took Ita a split-second or two to comprehend that her mam was humming. Humming happily, more to the point.

'You're in good form, Mam.' She stared at her quizzically.

Kate slipped the dress she'd just shaken out onto a coat hanger. 'Shall I tell you a secret, Ita?'

'Go on then.' Of course, Ita had no idea what was coming, but whatever it was, it was having a remarkable effect on her mam's mood.

'Chris isn't married.'

'But he wears a wedding ring?' Ita was bewildered both by the animated girlishness on her mam's face and the revelation she'd shared.

'It's all a ruse. The ring was his late dad's. He only wears it to avoid complications of the romantic kind with certain members of the choir.'

Ita's mouth fell open.

'You can't blame the man. He's handsome, and he said the last choir he directed disbanded over an altercation involving three sopranos who'd decided he was the fellow for them.'

'Why did he tell you then?' Ita asked, bewildered.

Kate gave a slight shrug. 'He said he feels he can be honest with me.'

'But he hardly knows you, Mam.' Christ on a bike, was she hearing this?

'Ita, sometimes between two people there's an instant connection.'

Ita rubbed at her ears.

'Close your mouth, Ita. I might be a woman of a certain age, but that doesn't mean I'm past my prime.'

Had the world gone mad? Connections and not past her prime were not phrases the mam Ita knew would ever use.

'Oh, and in between performances, we're to visit the Cliffs of Mohr. I've always wanted to see them.'

'All of us?' Ita asked weakly.

'No, just Chris and myself.' Kate shot her daughter a look that said that should be obvious.

Ita had to sit down. The mattress springs protested at her weight.

'Sure, Ita, if you opened your eyes instead of moping about the place, you'd see a fella who's waiting for you to notice him. Get him to take you to see the cliffs.' Kate carried on blithely, putting her clothes away.

Ita was stumped. Who was she on about? Please not Martin with the dandruff and rumbly baritone voice so at odds with his small stature. She had caught him looking her way more than once.

Kate's tone was exasperated. 'Oisin, Ita. He's smitten with you. It's plain as day.'

Ita was glad she was seated. Oisin? She fancied him obviously, but he'd not given her any clues he might feel the same. Or had he? Her mind raked over all the evenings spent at Madigan's. But no, there was nothing there to hint he might be interested in her. Then, she recalled the concern she'd seen when she'd confided her mam was digging her heels in over the festival. The way he'd made Kate Finnegan laugh in a carefree manner Ita hadn't witnessed in years. Even her mam humming and being here in Lisdoonvarna was down to him. And what about him winning Snuffy over? He was special, alright, but did he think she was too? She thought about how kind his eyes were behind his glasses and the unruly lock of hair that insisted on flopping into his eyes. Her heart began to race in a silly fashion.

'You think he likes me?' Ita half-whispered, not daring to believe it.

'I think you're the only one who hasn't noticed he can hardly take his eyes off you.'

Ita had never thought of herself as the sort of girl who fellas struggled to tear their eyes away from. 'Well, if he is interested in me like that, then why hasn't he done anything about it?' She was struggling to believe what her mam was saying. And besides, wouldn't Mags have said something to her if she'd noticed Oisin gawping at her.

'Oh, Ita. Why do you think? You've not given him any reason to. You walk about with your head in the clouds and a miserable expression on your face.'

This wasn't true. Or maybe it was? The head in the clouds part at least; as for the miserable expression, she didn't, did she? And what could she do about it?

'What should I do, Mam?'

'Do you like him?'

'I think I do, yes.'

'Well now, aren't we here at the matchmaking festival?'

'Yes, but—'

'But nothing, Ita. I think it would be perfectly acceptable if you were to ask Oisin to one of the dances we saw going on on the way in.'

'Mam, I couldn't.' Ita shook her head vehemently.

'Ita, life's too short for shoulda, coulda, woulda. G'won with you now and ask him out.' Oh, and, Ita...'

'Yes?'

'Smile for the love of God.'

Chapter Twenty-six

'Quiet, girls, quiet the weather's after coming on.' Maureen flapped her hand at her three daughters from the kitchen, then turned the radio up.

'It won't be any different to an hour ago, Mammy.' Roisin spoke over the top of the newsreader blanching at the sight of her mahogany mammy. Moira had prewarned them as she drove them to Howth that Mammy had gone to the beauty salon for the latest tanning fad, the Tropic. The idea was to be glowing for the party, as though a sun-kissed week in Hawaii had been had. But, instead, she'd walked out of the salon with the Victoria Beckham after a month in Ibiza look. Moira advised them not to say a word as she was a mammy on the edge over the party.

Roisin and Noah had arrived first thing that morning, with Shay picking them up from Dublin airport. She'd high hopes of running into O'Mara's and offloading her son, Mr Nibbles, and Steve on his aunts so as she could head round to Shay's for the riding.

Aisling and Moira had told her to forget it. Mammy had summoned them, and according to them, she'd used 'the voice'. Rosi had explained this to a disappointed Shay because when Mammy used 'the voice', you hopped to. So they'd arranged to meet up later.

Rosi had been itching to pick up her niece from the moment she'd arrived, but Mammy had other ideas. She'd made a fuss of Noah and commented on how well Mr Nibbles was looking now he had a, ahem, friend. Then it was Roisin's turn to be kissed and hugged. 'You're too thin,

Rosi,' she decided after giving her the once over. 'I'll soon fix that. Now then, where's the Mo-pants?' Roisin handed over the bag of stretchy pants bought in bulk from a London market.

'I'll deal with them later,' Maureen muttered, carting them off to the guest bedroom. Her face when she returned, meant business. 'Right. You've one hundred paper flowers to be cracking on with. Rosi, you're in charge.' She'd handed Roisin an origami book she'd found at the library.

A thick wad of coloured paper and glue, along with scissors, were already set out on the table.

Roisin and Aisling had done their best not to mention the elephant in the room—Mammy's mahogany face— because it was as Moira had said. She was indeed a Mammy on the edge. So, not daring to do otherwise, they'd dutifully snipped, folded and glued, trying not to take umbrage at Roisin's bossy instructions.

Now, while Maureen strained to hear the radio, Roisin was alongside her in the kitchen, tipping what was left of her mammy's basmati rice into one of Kiera's bottles. Aisling and Moira were tidying up the origami flower debris. The table was a mass of colourful paper flowers.

Aisling looked over at her mammy who had begun to pace back and forth. 'Jaysus wept, Mammy, calm down, would you? You're obsessed, so you are. Watch this space,' she said to her sisters. 'She's fancied herself a long-in-the-tooth weathergirl ever since she moved here. She'll be saying things like we're in for atmospheric indigestion, squally showers and Arctic blasts soon.'

Moira and Roisin sniggered.

'I'm good at the short-range, but I've not mastered the long-range forecast yet, and, Aisling O'Mara, don't tempt fate,' Maureen admonished. The whites of her eyes were sharp against her unnaturally tanned face as she flicked a panicked glance to the drizzly vista outside. Her prized sea view was a panorama of grey. It was the day before the party and the weekend forecast was not good. She'd been praying for a miracle all week, but so far, Him upstairs had been ignoring her. A tiki bar in the rain with sodden tropical origami flowers was not part of the plan.

'O'Mara-Moran, Mammy,' Aisling replied automatically.

Moira, spying what Roisin was up to with the rice, said, 'What are you planning on doing with that? You can't be giving a five-month-old uncooked rice. Jaysus, Rosi, how did Noah ever survive?'

'We live in a disposable world, Moira,' Roisin said, setting the bottle down and gesturing to the box of toys Maureen kept on hand for Kiera's visits. 'And why? What's it all for? Kiera will get as much enjoyment out of this as she will any of those.'

'Feck off with yourself, Rosi,' Moira said. 'You've got a box twice that size of Lego for Noah at home. And you're always giving out about having trod on the stuff.'

Rosi didn't deign to answer that as she set about screwing the lid on the bottle.

Moira eyed her sister as she ventured back into the living room and picked up Kiera with the lid now firmly on the rice-filled bottle. Roisin shook the bottle and Kiera giggled, grabbing for it. And so it went. She was right, Moira thought, Kiera loved it. Not that she'd admit it to her sister. She was already a fecky-know-it-all.

'Mum, Mr Nibbles is dive-bombing Steve again,' Noah yelled from where he was lying on his stomach on the floor near the French doors rolling a ball for Pooh to fetch and bring back.

'That fecking gerbil.' Roisin made no move to get up as she shook the shaker.

'Roisin, if my granddaughter's first word is fecking, there'll be murder. I've already had words with Moira over her using the bad language around the babby Kiera. And you two can stop smirking and all. You've five minutes break, and then it's into the kitchen with the lot of youse.' If Donal got back with the shopping, she'd sent him out for. She checked the wall clock, and her blood pressure surged.

The party food prep was a herculean undertaking that needed to be got on with now. Maureen had decided anything that could be made in advance was to be whipped up today. She had her list, and she'd assigned each of her daughters a job, so they didn't start fighting in the kitchen over the least taxing task. Even Noah had a designated job. He was on the washing of the vegetables. If Pooh could be trusted around food, he'd have been given something to do too.

'Mum!' Noah yelled once more. Pooh woofed.

'I told you to leave Mr Nibbles and Steve with your dad, Noah. He brought Steve into the fold. So it's up to him to manage Mr Nibbles' antisocial behaviour.' Roisin spoke sharply, her usual yoga Zennishness deserting her.

'It's a madhouse, so it is.' Maureen threw her hands up. 'And where's Donal? He should be back by now. Time's marching on. I didn't ask him to buy the whole supermarket, just the fruit and vegetables. He can never stick to a shopping list.'

'Ah, now, Mammy, don't be giving out to the poor man. It's not his fault the forecast for Saturday is for the squally showers and you're after inviting half of Dublin around for a luau.' Moira felt a loyal surge towards her mammy's man friend.

The door opened then and Donal appeared. He was a sorry sight, dripping wet and weighed down by shopping bags. The leaves of a pineapple tuft protruded from one shopping bag, and an enormous watermelon took up space in another.

'The supermarket was mad busy. Anyone would think it was the Thursday before Good Friday. And, would you believe, there was only one watermelon in the whole place. I might have dislocated my shoulder snatching it before anyone else got to it.'

'Do you think you'll still be able to turn the chicken wings on the barbeque tomorrow?' Maureen's brow crinkled.

Donal dumped the shopping bags and rotated his shoulder. 'It's a little sore.'

Aisling, Roisin and Moira waited for her to start singing the 'Solider On' song, but she didn't. It was most unfair.

'You'll be grand. Put it all behind you now, Donal. Sure, you're back and in one piece. Go and dry yourself off before you catch a chill. I'll put the Deep Heat on it later for you.'

Donal duly took himself off in the direction of their bedroom.

'Girls, don't just sit about looking gormless, get off your arses! C'mon, you can help too, Noah.'

The three sisters all raised their eyebrows. Mammy never used words like arse. Aisling, who'd been about to say how come Donal wasn't subjected to the 'Soldier On' song, thought better of it as, in an unspoken agreement, they decided it would be wise to do as they were told. Kiera began to wail as she was plopped on the ground, and the source of her fun got to her feet and walked away.

Nobody knew Noah had taken Mr Nibbles out of the cage to chastise him, but the gerbil had wriggled free. Noah, looking up at his nana, who was being bossy with himself and his aunts decided now wasn't the time to say anything.

Chapter Twenty-seven

Ita worked her way in and around the people standing shoulder to shoulder as they laughed, talked and clinked pint glasses. The atmosphere was smoky and festive inside O'Shea's, but she was oblivious to this or the tradition charm of the pub she'd arranged to meet Mags in.

Her mind was buzzing over the conversation she'd had with her mam because things were not going as she'd planned. So much for whisking Kate Finnegan away under a pretext she'd yet to think of to the Matchmaker Bar. Instead, her mam had headed off with Chris to explore the village; not before having given her a romance pep talk, which all things considered was a tad hypocritical given Kate Finnegan's refusal to move on from her ex-husband all these years.

Move on, it would appear, she was at long last doing though. Her mam's speech about life being too short for having regrets over missed moments had resonated, and Ita had left the hotel determined to be brave.

She'd throw caution to the wind and ask Oisin if he'd like to come to one of the evening's many dances. She'd seen them advertised in the windows of the pubs on their way into town. What was the worst thing that could happen? she asked herself, scanning the packed space for him and Mags. Don't answer that, she ordered herself as mortifying rejection sprang to mind. There was no sign of either of them.

Alice must have felt like this when she stepped through the looking glass, Ita decided, muttering an apology as she knocked some fella's elbow, and his drink sloshed. The world felt out of kilter, but she also felt strangely optimistic that the next three days here in Lisdoonvarna might prove to be the best in her life.

Sure, look at the start they were off to with her mam and Chris getting on so famously! She'd never have thought it. Not in a million years, but there was magic about, that was for sure. Narrowly missing the glowing tip of a cigarette a girl was waving about, Ita hoped a little of that magic came her way.

A flash of unnaturally white hair caught her eye, and Ita stood on tippy toes. It was Mags up near the bar and she homed in on her. Her friend was in lively conversation with a lad with an equally interesting hairstyle and nose piercing. There was no sign of Oisin though she saw, wondering where he'd got to. A smile broke across Mags's face seeing Ita approach, and as she drew close, she reached out and pulled her into their huddle.

'Ita, this is Aidan, Aidan, Ita. Aidan's from Galway here for the craic like.'

Aidan raised his nearly empty pint glass at her. He was good looking, Ita thought, once you got past the hair, piercings and tattoos. Right up Mags's alley. She smiled her hello. Then turned to Mags, 'Have you seen Oisin?'

'I saw him in the lobby before I came here. He said he had something he needed to do. He knows where we are.' She shrugged.

Aidan drained his glass and checked out Mags's glass which was also nearly empty. 'Can I get you girls a drink?'

'I'm grand, thanks. I only called in to tell Mags I'm off to find someone,' Ita replied.

'Isn't that why we're all here?' Aidan grinned, turning away and pushing forward for the bar.

Mags leaned in towards Ita. 'He's so cute, and he loves the fifties like me. He's got every Elvis movie ever made on DVD.'

That explained Aidan's rockabilly hairstyle then, Ita thought, taking in Mags's sparkling eyes and flushed cheeks. 'It didn't take you long to find your match.' She grinned then added, 'I can't stick around. I need to find Oisin.'

'Oisin, eh?' Mags raised her dark brows, studying Ita intently for a moment.

'What?'

'It's about time you two realised you're made for each other.'

Ita was stunned. 'Mam's not long said the same thing. Why didn't you say something to me if you thought that?'

'You're a closed book, Ita. You don't invite those sorts of conversations. I'd say that's why poor Oisin's never taken the next step and asked you out.'

'Did he say that?'

'Didn't have to.'

Ita thought about what Mags had said. Was she a closed book? There was truth in it, she supposed because she did hold herself back. It was the fear of being hurt, of being rejected. She was frightened of experiencing the sort of pain she'd felt when her dad had stopped being part of her life. 'I don't mean to be like that.'

'Ah, sure you're grand.' Mags had already moved on, as was her way. She was a plain speaker, was all. 'And what about your mam and Chris?' She broke into a rendition of 'Love is in the Air'.

Ita laughed, 'It's this place. I tell you it's mad.'

Mags gave her a push. 'So, go. Do something mad. Find Oisin and ask him out.'

'Should I?'

'Definitely.'

Ita bit her lip. This was her moment, her chance. She wasn't going to waste it. 'I'll catch you later then.' She wove her way back from where she'd come.

The crisp afternoon air was a relief after the stuffy pub, and she gulped at it before allowing herself to be swept along the pavement with the crowd. The high spirits were infectious and she felt giddy as she was carried along in no particular direction. But where on earth should she start looking for him? Ita wondered, feeling her earlier elation at taking love into her own hands evaporate at the sight of so many people. He could be in a pub, at a restaurant, or even at a dance for all she knew. Or maybe he was already back at the hotel. Perhaps she should head back there.

As it happened, she didn't have to look for him.

Oisin found her.

Ita nearly tripped over her own feet as up ahead, moving through the thronging crowd, she saw a sign bobbing about over the tops of the heads of the revellers. She read the words then reread them to be sure she wasn't hallucinating.

Ita, say yes to a date!

It couldn't be, could it? Maybe the message was meant for another Ita. She couldn't see who was holding the sign and someone protested as she elbowed past them, not apologising in her haste. She ducked and dived, keeping her eyes trained on the sign until, at last, only one person was coming between her and whoever was holding it aloft.

'Excuse me,' she spoke up, desperate to move the burly fella with a rugby player's neck who was blocking her path aside. He moved to the left, and there he was, Oisin.

'Ita,' he stopped short.

'Oisin.'

'Now youse two know each other's names would you mind moving out the way?' A girl with orange-tinted foundation clutching a helium heart balloon demanded.

Oisin reached out and took Ita's elbow. 'Follow me.'

She let herself be pulled off the street and into a nearby restaurant. They stood staring at one another, and then Ita was dimly aware of a waiter moving towards them. He stopped short and turned to a passing waitress balancing a platter of cheese, crackers and grapes. 'Here we go again. Another pair of star-crossed lovers. It's the same every year.'

'Will you?' Oisin's expression was serious as he pushed his glasses up on his nose. He jiggled his sign. 'I had it made especially. It was yer matchmaker man's idea.'

'You went to see him?'

'I did, and I touched his magic book with my eyes closed for eight seconds and envisaged love.

'Well, then I have to say yes to a date.' The smile Ita gave Oisin shook away the vestiges of discontent to reveal the pretty girl buried inside. She knew from this moment forth, Oisin was going to be someone special in her life.

The waiter and waitress, along with several diners within earshot, gave them a round of applause.

Chapter Twenty-eight

The Party

'Welcome, welcome,' Maureen called out across the living room, waving madly at Amanda and Terence, who'd appeared in the entrance. The couple were decked out in summery outfits with matching panama hats and were fashionably late.

Maureen eyed Bold Brenda, on whom she'd been keeping a strict eye since she'd arrived earlier minus Niall. Their fellow rambler, whom Brenda won over with the gourmet trail mix, was away visiting family for the weekend she'd informed Maureen. Then, checking Rosemary and Cathal Carrick, the cobbler, were out of earshot she'd begun angling for the inside scoop on Howth's hottest new couple. The invitation to join in with the Howth ramblers had done the trick.

As such, Maureen had no qualms cutting her off mid-sentence to go and announce her neighbours' arrival. A gossip she was not.

Amanda and Terence were the sorta couple who'd expect to be announced at parties, she decided. The sort who liked to make a splash. She made her excuses to Brenda and, reaching for her crutches, hopped towards the couple.

It was a sixth sense that made her pause and turn to look back over her shoulder. Lo and behold, Brenda had made a beeline for the tiki bar outside once more.

God had smiled down on Maureen this day because, at four pm, the rain clouds had dispersed, and the sun had decided to shine down. He wasn't smiling down upon her now, though, because she was just after dragging Brenda back inside the house. So, spying Moira, who was jiggling Kiera on her hip as she laughed about something with her old pal, Andrea and new friends, Mona and Lisa, she decided to charge her with the task of keeping Brenda indoors.

Her youngest child looked fetching but, more importantly, decent in a sky blue sarong. She'd knotted it into a halterneck dress of sorts. It was a vast improvement on the shorts overtop her swimsuit she'd been wearing when she arrived—if you could call them shorts. They were more like the rompers Aisling used to wear for the cross country all those years ago, only in silver.

Maureen had blocked her daughter's entrance to the house when the family of three had arrived an hour before the party was due to get underway. She'd told her daughter in no uncertain terms what she thought of the shorty-pants.

'I can see what you had for breakfast in those, Moira O'Mara'

'So? They're all the rage since Kylie wore the hot pants in that music video of hers. And I want to show off my post-baby figure.' Moira was unrepentant as she struck a pose on the front doorstep.

Tom placed an approving hand on Moira's derriere but removed it swiftly when Maureen fixed him with the hairy eyeball.

She'd pulled her daughter inside. 'Get in before the neighbours see you making a holy show of yourself. I don't care what Kylie's after wearing. I'm not her mammy, now am I? And I say, you'll not be sharing your toasted buns with my guests, thank you very much. There's a sarong on the back of my bedroom door.' She knew her daughters well enough to guess one of them would ignore her strict dress code instructions. Hence the emergency sarong. No surprises it was Moira.

'But, Mammy!'

'But Mammy nothing, Moira,' she'd thundered, meaning business. 'You'll put it on if you know what's good for you.'

Moira had scuttled off to do as she was told. They'd already had words over Kiera's outfit, with Maureen pumping for the pink frills and Moira gunning for green dungarees. In the end, Tom had intervened, telling them both in no uncertain terms, he would decide what his daughter wore to the party. He'd done well dressing her in a yellow dress with white daisies and a matching sun hat. Maureen would have preferred the pink frills, but who was she to comment? She was only the child's maternal nana, after all.

Now, she prodded her daughter with one of her crutches. She was beginning to understand why Rosemary was so fond of her hiking pole. It came in handy.

'Ow, Mammy, don't be prodding me.' Moira swung around.

It was Maureen's turn to be unrepentant. 'We have a situation.'

Moira rubbed her backside. 'What situation?' She scanned the room, eyes narrowed, wondering if Aisling had fallen out of her top as she was apt to do. But, no, there was her sister helping Quinn in the kitchen with both bosoms safely contained inside her strappy sundress. She'd been in fits earlier, catching sight of her brother-in-law's white legs protruding from his surfie-style board shorts. Aisling had offered to put the fake tan on him, but he'd declined, having seen Maureen's new 'I've just spent a month sunbathing on the Continent' look.

'Bold Brenda over there in the wispy chiffon number is a moth to the flame where the tiki bar's concerned. Look-it there she goes again asking Tom for a refill,' Maureen said.

Tom had volunteered for the job of barman. He'd been channelling Tom Cruise from cocktail much to the delight of the quilting ladies. They'd been flocking around him, and when Maureen brought Kiera over to say hello to them all, she'd interrupted them ordering things like a Sex on the Beach and a Harvey Wallbanger. One thing was sure. When Tom qualified and began practising as a GP, he'd never be short of females keen to discuss their various ailments with Doctor Tom.

'And why's that a problem?' Moira raked her eyes over the plump woman. She was slightly older than her mammy and wearing a dress designed for a twenty-year-old. Moira frowned, watching her elbowing the group of ladies in their summery three-quarter length trousers, all pulled up to their armpits, out the way. Hang on a tick, what on earth was she wearing under her dress?

'Because, Moira, when she's standing in the light, that dress of hers is see-through. And, she's after squeezing into the tighty-whities again.'

'Ah, Jaysus! I'd better rescue Tom. Sure that could put him off the riding for life,' Moira sprang into action, thrusting Kiera at Andrea before hot-footing it outside.

'And while you're at it, Moira, tell Tom to tone it down. Norma there in the sparkly blue top and white capris has a heart condition.'

Bold Brenda was standing on tippy toes now she'd pushed her way to the bar trying to check out the tiki barman's bottom as he bent over to retrieve another bottle of rum to add to the fruit punch. Moira appeared at her side and hauled her into the house. 'I've someone you should meet, Bold, I mean Brenda.'

'But what about my drink—'

Her cry fell on deaf ears.

Maureen, seeing Bold Brenda offloaded onto Randy Rory from the yacht club, was satisfied the situation had been contained. She carried on over to where her neighbours were still wafting about uncertainly on the edge of the room.

'Amanda, Terence! Hello there, so glad you could make it.' She did the air-kissing and was a little taken aback when Terence turned his head and caught her on the lips. It took some effort not to wipe her mouth with the back of her hand because it had been a not very neighbourly wet sorta kiss.

'You're looking extremely well there, Maureen. That's some colour you're after getting. Amanda didn't mention you and Donal had been away? Spain was it, Tenerife maybe?' He gestured to her crutches. 'Doing the limbo were you and got carried away?' A chortle at his little joke followed.

Maureen managed a polite titter. 'Not at all. I tripped over, and it's a homegrown tan from walking Pooh along the pier, Terence. I've the second summer we're after having to thank for it.' The white lie had been trotted out more than once this evening as she fended off enquires into her bronze appearance.

Amanda gave Maureen a sceptical once over, but she looked beyond their hostess to the living room and garden. 'Goodness me, Maureen, it's standing room only. Did you invite all these people?'

'I, well, sorta, yes.' Maureen was starting to feel antsy about the numbers that had been trickling in the door and had been avoiding catching Donal's eye. The hibiscus flowers were long gone, as were the leis, although she'd held two back specifically for Amanda and Terence. Maureen scanned the living room and beyond to the garden, catching sight of Ciara with a 'C'. The lad with the fluff on his chin beside her must be her boyfriend, she deduced. She was doing a grand job of making the girl from the Mothercare, whose name she couldn't remember, feel at home.

Yer Barbie and Ken couple from the end of the trio of converted townhouses comprising Mornington Mews, Owen and Tanya had cornered Aisling's friend Leila. They were picking her brains about weddings in case they ever decided to tie the knot. She was glad Leila and Aisling had patched things up. Her daughter needed her friends right now.

Outside, the golfing girls demonstrated putting techniques to Bernadette, whom Maureen had met on the pier. Her fellow line dancing ladies and Laura, their instructor, were mixing and mingling and the senior Mr and Mrs Moran were chatting to the Dalys. She spied Bronagh admiring the special heel on Rosemary's sandal that Cathal had presented her with on their second date. Maureen supposed that's what you got when you stepped out with a cobbler.

Meanwhile, Roisin and Shay were doing a superb job of passing the canapés around although she wished Shay had opted for a tee shirt. The singlet he was parading about in showed all his tattoos off.

There were a few other faces Maureen recognised vaguely but couldn't have told you where from. Yer man over there might have worked at the petrol station, but she couldn't be sure.

Oh, and there was Louise and the family. Donal's other daughter Anna had created a stir arriving hand in hand with her friend, Helen. Donal had necked his drink as it dawned on him who it was that had been making his workaholic daughter smile of late. He was liberally minded though was Donal, like herself. It was one of the many things Maureen loved about him. Each to their own and live and let live was their motto.

'Sure,' he'd said, 'the world's a different place to what it was when we grew up, Mo, and if yer woman over there makes Anna happy, that's good enough for me.'

Maureen smiled fondly at her live-in, man friend then remembered what she'd hobbled over to do. 'Everybody.' The din in the room continued, and Maureen would have tapped the side of a glass with a spoon had she not been on the crutches.

She flapped her hand at Niall, The Gamblers' guitarist strumming the ukulele over in the corner. She'd ask Donal to have a quiet word because 'My Old Man's A Dustman' wasn't what she had in mind when she'd asked him to play the ukulele for them.

Niall, glad to take a break, stopped playing and went in search of a drink. Maureen tried again to get the room's attention, this time using the same tone she'd used on Moira earlier. It worked a treat, and all eyes turned towards her. 'Everybody, Amanda and Terence from next door have arrived.'

There was a murmuring of 'hello there' from the packed living room and one 'who cares' from a heckler Maureen couldn't locate in the milling crowd. Amanda and Terence waved like the royal couple on the balcony. When the commotion died down and people had returned once more to their conversations, Amanda asked how Maureen had come to trip over and wind up on crutches.

'Well now, it's only a twisted ankle, but it's the same one I broke in Vietnam a while back. Donal insisted on bandaging it up.' She'd thought she might have to bandage Donal's big toe, too, but the fungal toenail had cleared up in the nick of time. 'Would you believe I'm after tripping over my grandson's gerbil, Mr Nibbles? Noah let him out of the cage yesterday because he wouldn't stop bullying Steve, the new boy on the block with the lazy eye, and Mr Nibbles ran off. That's the culprit there.'

Amanda looked at the floor in horror before realising Maureen was gesturing outside to the lawn. Above the heads of the milling guests, paper flowers were strewn, and lanterns twinkled in the dusk. Thanks to those who'd taken the Hawaiian theme to the next level, the air smelled of coconut sun cream. Sun cream and booze. She could see Donal and a young boy waving tongs about by an enormous barbeque. The sight of the barbeque made her sigh. Terence wouldn't like that. It would be off to the outdoor living shops with him in the morning because he always had to have the biggest barbeque in the neighbourhood. She put it down to his erring on the short side.

'That's Noah there, helping Donal or Uncle Kenny as he's decided to call him with the chicken wings,' Maureen explained.

Amanda was struggling to keep up with all the names, and Terence had been too busy staring at Maureen's cleavage, showcased by a colourful lei, to pay any attention to what she'd been saying.

'Where was I?'

'Erm, an escaped gerbil.' Amanda's feet twitched inside their slingbacks. She'd an urge to stand on a chair because she'd yet to hear whether the gerbil had been caught.

'Yes, Mr Nibbles. He dashed out in front of me in a freedom run as I made my way to open the front door to yer woman dropping off the hibiscus flowers. I didn't stand a chance.' There was no need to go into the high drama that followed as she turned the air blue. She'd told Noah he'd best get hold of the rodent because if she got to him first, things would not end well for Mr Nibbles and Steve would find himself kingpin.

'And did you manage to capture this erm, Mr Nibbles?'

'Noah did yes. Mr Nibbles is currently in disgrace back at the guesthouse with Steve.'

Thank God for that, Amanda thought.

'Now then,' Maureen had had enough of the gerbil talk. 'We'll have you looking the part in no time. There's a lei for both of you in the kitchen and pink hibiscus for you,

Amanda. It'll look fetching with those flowers on your dress.'

Amanda, eager to make her escape, headed for the kitchen.

Once she was out of earshot, Maureen turned to Terence, intending to introduce him to Leila's Bearach, who was looking bored by the wedding chatter. She stopped short, however, seeing him giving her that peculiar smile once more. And for whatever reason, he was waving a pineapple keychain not dissimilar to the one she'd dropped around to their place with a spare key attached. 'You've got the pineapple keychain too, I see. And very nice it is too,' she offered up, unsure why he was waving it in her face.

'You smell wonderful, Maureen.' He leered, leaning dangerously close to her cleavage.

Funny, Maureen thought, taking a nervous step back, she'd never noticed how short he was. She was beginning to regret the plunging neckline of the wrap dress despite Donal's appreciation of her assets. She adjusted her lei in an attempt to hide her bosom, mumbling, 'It's Arpège you're after smelling. My signature perfume.'

'I saw the pink flamingo by the door.' He gave her an exaggerated wink.

'Oh, the flamingo. That was Donal's idea. You know, to let people know where the party was.'

Donal had indeed spotted it at the pound shop, and while Maureen wasn't sure if there were flamingos in Hawaii or not, she did know relationships were all about compromise. Hence, the plastic, pink flamingo had taken up residence at the entrance to the house.

'Amanda was saying only the other day what an attractive man Donal is.'

'Was she?' Maureen's eyebrows shot up.

'Yes, you're both rather attractive.'

'Well, now thanks a million. You'll have to excuse me. Aisling needs me in the kitchen.'

Maureen hobbled away as fast as she could, taking a wide berth around Amanda, who now had a flower behind her ear and a lei around her neck as she went in search of her husband. Aisling was buttering the bread rolls at the kitchen worktop.

'Holy God above tonight,' she gasped, reaching the safety of her daughter.

'What's got you flapping?' Aisling enquired, looking up from her task and noting how red her mammy was underneath the brown.

'I'm after having an unnerving encounter with Terence from next door.'

'In what way?' The butter knife was abandoned as Aisling raised an eyebrow.

Maureen relayed what had transpired, telling Aisling about Terence's odd behaviour with the pineapple key ring and his wink regarding the plastic, pink flamingo. When she finished, instead of the support she was seeking, she saw Aisling's shoulders shaking.

'Aisling O'Mara, it's not a laughing matter!'

'O'Mara-Moran, Mammy, and it is funny. Oh my God, it's so funny! Wait until I tell Moira and Rosi. They'll be crying.'

Quinn was looking at his wife quizzically. 'I don't get it either. What's so funny?'

Aisling, who was in fits, managed to gasp, 'A flamingo out the front of a house is the sign of a swingers house. So is a pineapple keychain.' She leaned into Quinn, her body quaking as she snorted in a most unladylike manner. 'Ah Jaysus, Mammy, yer neighbours are swingers! And they think you and Donal are too.'

Maureen's hand flew to her heart. 'Swingers? Like those frisky people who'd drop their keys in an ashtray at parties back in the seventies? Then go home with the wrong husband or wife.' She forgot all about how she'd been congratulating herself and Donal on their liberal mindedness earlier in the evening and their motto of live and let live.

Aisling nodded, wiping at her eyes. 'Has my mascara run?' she asked Quinn.

He shook his head and then waggled his eyebrows. 'What I want to know, Ash, is how come you're such an authority on the subject?'

Aisling swatted him. 'I don't have first-hand experience. I read all about it in a bonkbuster.'

'A Jilly Cooper?' Maureen said knowingly, slowly recovering her equilibrium.

'I can't remember, but I remember the pineapples and flamingos.'

Maureen's mouth puckered in that way it did when she meant business, and turning away from Aisling and Quinn, she marched off.

'Where are you off to, Mammy?' Aisling called after her.

Maureen looked back over her shoulder and said grimly, 'I've a flamingo to be dealing with.'

Chapter Twenty-nine

'Encore, encore, encore!' The chant rang out on the night air across the Howth hillside. The Gamblers had finished their second forty-minute set with Kenny Roger's 'Daytime Lovers'. The line dancing crew, Maureen included, had taken their places on the lawn in front of the open French doors where the band had set up inside. Laura, their instructor in her trademark white Stetson, had them following her lead as they performed the Tush Push for the partygoers. Judging by the applause and whistles, it had gone over well.

'What do you say, fellas?' Donal said to his bandmates. 'Have we got one more song in us?'

Niall, whose fingers were sore from the ukulele strumming, wasn't sure, but the other band members gave the nod.

'I'm going to need a little help up here though.' Donal bent down and retrieved the tambourine he'd bought Maureen not long after they'd begun stepping out together. He gave it a shake. 'What do you say, Maureen?'

'Maureen, Maureen, Maureen!'

Maureen, puffing and panting from the Tush Push, flushed beneath her tan not only from exertion but pleasure too. The crowd was going mad for her! This was her moment! She'd get her second wind, she determined, stepping up alongside Donal.

'Let's hear it for your hostess with the mostess, Maureen O'Mara!'

The applause was thunderous, and Maureen took her tambourine from Donal, gave it an appreciative shake, and did a twirl in her wrap dress. Then, as the clapping died down, the opening notes of 'Islands in the Stream' sounded, and a few 'Wahoos!' went up.

Maureen and Donal angled towards each other to share the microphone, and the chemistry between was plain for all to see. He was Kenny, and she was Dolly.

A few couples took to the floor to sway together to the music. Rosi gathered her sisters, and they draped an arm across each other's shoulders as they too rocked gently to the song.

'They're not bad,' Roisin said. There was wonderment in her tone, having never seen her mammy perform with Donal before.

'If you close your eyes, you could almost imagine it was Dolly Parton and Kenny Rogers up there,' Aisling added.

'The state of Mammy's cleavage, she'd give Dolly a run for her money,' Moira said. She swung around at a tap on her shoulder. They'd all heard the Amanda and Terence story and were keeping a wary distance from the couple. She relaxed, seeing it was Tom. He'd been inside keeping a watchful eye on Kiera, who'd nodded off in her car seat.

'Moira, the Hawaiian entertainment is after arriving. She's in the living room.'

'What time is it?'

'Nearly eleven.'

Moira blinked. The evening had whizzed by and had been a roaring success, although Mammy had voiced concern before the line dancing display about how well Bold Brenda and Randy Roy were getting on with Amanda and Terence. Noah, too, was fed up and had been making this known to his mother. All the food had long since been demolished, and he was coming down from the sugar high the numerous glasses of Coke he'd sneaked had given him. It was why he'd taken the news that the Hawaiian entertainment was not going to be a fire eater but rather a hula dancer badly. His daddy had told him all good luaus had a fire-eating display.

'I'll tell Mammy. How's Kiera?'

'Still sound asleep.'

'Moira?'

'Yeah?'

'She doesn't look very Hawaiian.'

'Is she in a grass skirt?'

'Yes?'

'Then she'll be grand.'

Tom gave her an uncertain smile and sidled back inside.

Maureen and Donal's duet came to a close, and Moira took the opportunity to tell her mammy in between her numerous curtsies and bows to her appreciative audience that the hula dancer she'd booked was here.

Maureen nudged Donal out of the way and commandeered the microphone. 'To round off this evening's entertainment, we've got a special treat in store for you. So charge your glasses and don't go anywhere.'

Maureen left Donal and the boys to pack up their equipment while she moseyed in to introduce herself to the hula dancer.

A young woman wearing a grass skirt with twin coconut shells barely covering her generous assets was sitting on the sofa with a boom box by her feet. A fake orange lei was draped around her neck, and a pink one encircled her head. Her hair was too black to be natural with a blue sheen to it under the light, and she'd slapped her makeup on with a trowel. As for her tan, Maureen fancied they might have visited the same salon.

'Hello there, I'm Maureen O'Mara. You must be from Hollywood Nights Party Entertainment.'

'Yeah, Chantel, where do you want me?' She snapped the gum she was chewing.

Maureen gestured to where the band was. 'As soon as they've cleared the space, you'll be up.'

'Grand.'

'Are they real coconut shells?' Maureen asked.

'No, they're from the pound shop.'

A conversation about the merits of the pound shop when it came to leis and the like ensued, and then, seeing the area was cleared, Maureen said, 'Come on then, Chantel, I'll introduce you to our guests.'

Maureen stood in the living room looking out at her packed lawn to where the sounds of merrymaking rang out. The lanterns had been a nice touch, twinkling in the darkness. Donal had packed the microphone away, so she had to shout to be heard, but she used 'the tone' again and soon had all eyes upon her.

'I said we'd got a special treat, and here she is. From Hawaii. Put your hands together for Chantel.' Another white lie, and Chantel was as exotically Polynesian sounding as Maureen but sure, where was the harm.

Clapping and a wolf whistle erupted. Maureen pursed her lips. She'd put money on the culprit being Randy Roy. Then she stepped down onto the lawn to let Chantel take centre stage.

Chantel pushed play on the boom box, and the Hukilau song began to play. Her hips began to sway, and her hands twirled gracefully to the left and then the right as her bare feet took tiny steps to the gentle hula song. Anklets adorned her slender ankles.

'Look at the abs on her, would yer,' Mona said to Moira. 'Maybe we should start a hula dancing club for new mams to get us back in shape.'

Suddenly the music that evoked images of balmy breezes, white-capped waves on a blue sea, cocktails and tropical nights stopped. Instead, Def Leopard's 'Pour Some Sugar on Me' blared from the boom box, a collective gasp sounded.

'I didn't know Def Leopard was Hawaiian,' Mona shouted.

Chantel whipped off her grass skirt to reveal an itsy-bitsy-teeny-weeny red bikini bottom. She strutted back and forth before gyrating in a slow circle giving the Howth housewarming party guests an eyeful of two plump peach cheeks.

'Christ on a bike,' Aisling muttered to no one in particular. 'Mammy's after booking a stripper!'

As Chantel began to fiddle with the string holding her coconut cups in place, Maureen leapt into action, prodding the scantily clad young woman with her crutch. Chantel, startled, backed away as the crutch kept jabbing at her. Someone booed as she disappeared into the depths of the living room, with Maureen hobbling inside in hot-pursuit.

Donal hit stop on the boom box and, over the excited chatter of their guests, announced there'd been a misunderstanding.

Meanwhile, Maureen having jabbed Chantel all the way to the sofa told her to stay right there while she went and located another emergency sarong. She flapped it at the exotic dancer insisting she wrap it around her waist.

'I don't understand,' Chantel muttered keeping a wary eye on the crutch as she did as she was told. 'You booked me.'

'For the hula dancing, not the shaking your bonbons!'

Aisling, Moira and Rosi appeared in the living room clutching each other as they fell about the place.

'It's not a laughing matter.' Maureen repeated her earlier phrase as she shot them daggers. 'Excuse my daughters, pumpkin heads they might have, but they've got the brain of a pea between them.'

'No, it's not,' Chantel sniffed agreeing with Maureen as she saw her tips go up in smoke.

'Sorry, Mammy,' Roisin choked out, 'but you said you wanted to make your and Donal's housewarming a night nobody would forget. I think you outdid yourself.'

Chapter Thirty

Three Months Later

Ita was polishing the banister rail on the first floor of O'Mara's with the dreamy look on her face that meant she was thinking about Oisin—again.

He made her happy, and he'd helped her to mend bridges with her dad and Francine too. She'd never have had the courage to knock on their door if he hadn't been standing beside her squeezing her hand to let her know she wasn't alone.

She squirted the lemony spray, remembering the afternoon they'd walked up the stairs of the Ranelagh house she'd never visited to knock on the cheerful blue, Georgian door.

'I don't think I can do this, after all, Oisin,' Ita had said. Her legs were like jelly, and if he hadn't had a firm hold of her hand, she would have run down those steps and back down the leafy street to catch a bus to anywhere but where she currently was.

'You can, Ita. I'm here with you.' He squeezed her hand for good measure.

Ita took a deep breath and picked up the brass lion's head knocker. She rapped it three times, letting it fall back down, and then stepped back from the door.

After a few seconds, she said, 'I don't think anybody's home.' It was both a relief and a disappointment.

'Try again.'

Her expression as she looked up at Oisin said, Do I have to?

His told her they weren't going anywhere until she had.

Ita made to pick up the knocker once more, but her arm fell back by her side as the door suddenly swung open.

'Sorry, I was upstairs,' a breathy voice apologised. 'Oh.' Francine's eyes widened as she registered who was standing on her doorstep.

'Hello, Frankie,' Ita ventured uncertainly. She was surprised by how easy it was to use her dad's partner's nickname, after all. Would the door be slammed in her face? She couldn't read the other woman's expression. Francine didn't look much different. A little frazzled perhaps in that way mams sometimes did, and the high heels were gone having been replaced by flats. Oisin had told her she was best, to be honest, and get straight to the point of her visit, and this was what she did blurting, 'I've come to say I'm sorry for how I treated you, and I'd like the chance to spend time with my dad and to get to know you and the girls properly if you'd let me.'

'Who is it, Frankie?'

Ita's heart leapt as she heard a familiar voice she'd not heard in a long while.

'Ita!'

And there he was, her dad. A little slimmer these days, his hair a little thinner but unmistakably her dad. His face broke into a welcoming smile and Ita's legs steadied. She wouldn't be turned away.

'What are you doing standing there. Come in, come in.' He held the door open wide.

Before she could take a step toward the house, however, Francine blocked her way.

'You're very welcome,' Francine said, holding her arms out to embrace her.

Ita was enveloped in a hug that smelled of baking and coffee, and she returned it, clinging tightly to the woman she'd despised for no other reason than she thought she should. Tears over so much wasted time prickled, but there was no time for lamenting the past because her dad was shaking Oisin's hand heartily, and then they were ushered inside the house.

'Girls, look who's come to see us!' Francine had called out, and running footsteps had sounded.

Ita didn't realise she was smiling as she rubbed the duster up and down the rail. She smiled a lot these days. So did her mam. Thanks to Breda pulling out of Lisdoonvarna, her mam had met Chris and begun living again.

She regularly visited her dad, Frankie, and sisters and was beginning to feel a part of their family. It was her dad who'd talked her into enrolling on a part-time vet assistant course. One day soon, she'd hand her notice in here at O'Mara's and do what she should have done from the get-go.

Ita's daydreaming halted as Aisling thundered down the stairs, not registering Ita was there on the landing.

What was going on? Ita wondered, angling herself so she could hear what was happening below.

'Bronagh, Bronagh, look, two lines. I'm pregnant!'

The End.

Thanks so much for reading The Housewarming. If you enjoyed this latest instalment in the O'Mara family's lives please recommend the books to other readers and leave a review or starred rating on Amazon or Goodreads. I'd so appreciate it!

There are more O'Mara family shenanigans coming soon in...

Rainbows over O'Mara – Book 12, The Guesthouse on the Green series

Out July 2022 (if not earlier!)